Science Fiction Tales

Science Fiction Tales

Invaders, Creatures, and Alien Worlds

Edited by Roger Elwood

Introduction by Theodore Sturgeon

Illustrated by Rod Ruth

Rand McNally & Company

Chicago / New York / San Francisco

Library of Congress Cataloging in Publication Data

Elwood, Roger, comp.
Science fiction tales; invaders, creatures and alien worlds.
CONTENTS: McCaffrey, A. The smallest dragonboy.—Tofte, A. Alone in space.—Street, C. E. The mysterious gem. [etc.]
1. Science fiction. [1. Science fiction.
2. Short stories] I. Ruth, Rod, illus. II. Title.
PZ5.E48Sc [Fic] 73-9799
ISBN 0-528-82504-6
ISBN 0-528-82505-4 (lib. bdg.)

Printed in the United States of America
by Rand McNally & Company

First paperback printing, 1977

CONTENTS

introduction: the wonder-full age

by THEODORE STURGEON

Watching my two-year-old Andros carefully emptying a large drum of colored blocks on the living-room carpet twelve minutes after I had picked them all up, I began to think other than the usual thoughts: that children are disobedient slaves, or that they are super-geniuses, out to get you.

I was lying on the couch watching him, with my head propped up on one hand, and I thought: suppose . . . just suppose . . . that the couch should disappear, and that I should continue to lie as I was, on my side, head in hand, in midair.

Would Andros notice?

Providing I made no special outcry or movement, I am pretty sure he would make very little of it. He lives in a world that he is unable to explain. Indeed, the pressure to explain—the thing that drives most of the rest of us so cruelly—is not yet a part of his thoughts. He's in the business of collecting information, not of organizing it. He is registering hard, sweet, hot, sharp, bitter, fast, tickle, cold, hurt, but *how* and *why* are of very little concern to him. As a tiny infant he was doing the same data-gathering, of course, but there is now an important difference; he is not quietly feeling and reacting anymore. He is now charting an active course between these new and strange things, learning what to avoid and what to strive for. Still, his world is almost empty of *how* and *why;* it is a very real world—more real, perhaps, than yours or mine. It lacks, however, the sense of wonder. To see a man pull a rabbit and a bowl of goldfish and a Christmas tree out of a hat is not a mystery to him. There is no surprise, you sense no mystery, unless and until you wonder—wonder why, wonder how.

In a few weeks or months now, should my couch disappear and leave me calmly floating in midair, it will make a difference. Just how much would depend on Andros himself, but it's safe to say that a three-year-old and a four-year-old would, one way or another, demand an answer. And up through ages five and six, the answers would have to be increasingly precise and understandable, beginning with, "Well, Daddy just feels like it," through "All Daddys can do this" (I never said the explanation had to be true!), to "It's a magneto-gravitic field, son; I'll explain it when you're older." (Something we adults love to say.)

But beyond seven or eight and through twelve or thirteen, when Andros realizes that some phenomena are beyond his current ability to understand and he is bothered more and more by the powers of *why* and *how,* he will spice each answer he cannot understand with wonder. It is the sense of wonder which keeps the tool of curiosity whetted, just as it is imagination that sparks all invention, all human progress.

So it is that ages seven through thirteen are the most wonderful—wonder-full—of ages.

Science fiction is the myth and the fairy tale not of the past, but of the present and future—the places where you and Andros will live all your lives. Yet like the myth and the fairy tale, it preserves and enhances that almost indefinable sense of wonder.

And maybe, after you have finished these stories, you might like to recommend them to your parents. Who knows, you might find that their sense of wonder is a lot better than you thought it was.

the smallest dragonboy

by ANNE McCAFFREY

Although Keevan lengthened his walking stride as far as his legs would stretch, he couldn't quite keep up with the other candidates. He knew he would be teased again.

Just as he knew many other things that his foster mother told him he ought not to know, Keevan knew that Beterli, the most senior of the boys, set that spanking pace just to embarrass him, the smallest dragonboy. Keevan would arrive, tail fork-end of the group, breathless, chest heaving, and maybe get a stern look from the instructing wingsecond.

Dragonriders, even if they were still only hopeful candidates for the glowing eggs which were hardening on the hot sands of the Hatching Ground cavern, were expected to be punctual and prepared. Sloth was not tolerated by the weyrleader of Benden Weyr. A good record was especially important now. It was very near hatching time, when the baby dragons would crack their mottled shells and stagger forth to choose their lifetime companions. The very thought of that glorious moment made Keevan's breath catch in his throat. To be chosen—to be a dragonrider! To sit astride the neck of the winged beast with the jeweled eyes: to be his friend in telepathic communion with him for life; to be his companion in good times and fighting extremes; to fly effortlessly over the lands of Pern! Or, thrillingly, *between* to any point anywhere on the world! Flying *between* was done on dragonback or not at all, and it was dangerous.

Keevan glanced upward, past the black mouths of the weyr caves in which grown dragons and their chosen riders lived, toward the Star Stones that crowned the ridge of the old volcano that was Benden Weyr. On the height, the blue watch dragon, his rider mounted on his neck, stretched the great transparent pinions that carried him on the winds of Pern to fight the evil Thread that fell at certain times from the sky. The many-faceted rainbow jewels of his eyes glistened momentarily in the greeny sun. He folded his great wings to his back, and the watchpair resumed their statuesque pose of alertness.

Then the enticing view was obscured as Keevan passed into the Hatching Ground cavern. The sands underfoot were hot, even through heavy wher-hide boots. How the bootmaker had protested having to sew so small! Keevan was forced to wonder again why being small was reprehensible. People were always calling him "babe" and shooing him away as being "too small" or "too young" for this or that. Keevan was constantly working, twice as hard as any other boy his age, to prove himself capable. What if his muscles weren't as big as Beterli's? They were just as hard. And if he couldn't overpower anyone in a wrestling match, he could outdistance everyone in a footrace.

"Maybe if you run fast enough," Beterli had jeered on the occasion when Keevan had been goaded to boast of his swiftness, "you could catch a dragon. That's the only way you'll make a dragonrider!"

"You just wait and see, Beterli, you just wait," Keevan

had replied. He would have liked to wipe the contemptuous smile from Beterli's face, but the guy didn't fight fair even when the wingsecond was watching. "No one knows what Impresses a dragon!"

"They've got to be able to *find* you first, babe!"

Yes, being the smallest candidate was not an enviable position. It was therefore imperative that Keevan Impress a dragon in his first hatching. That would wipe the smile off every face in the cavern, and accord him the respect due any dragonrider, even the smallest one.

Besides, no one knew exactly what Impressed the baby dragons as they struggled from their shells in search of their lifetime partners.

"I like to believe that dragons see into a man's heart," Keevan's foster mother, Mende, told him. "If they find goodness, honesty, a flexible mind, patience, courage—and you've that in quantity, dear Keevan—that's what dragons look for. I've seen many a well-grown lad left standing on the sands, Hatching Day, in favor of someone not so strong or tall or handsome. And if my memory serves me" (which it usually did—Mende knew every word of every Harper's tale worth telling, although Keevan did not interrupt her to say so), "I don't believe that F'lar, our weyrleader, was all that tall when bronze Mnementh chose him. And Mnementh was the only bronze dragon of that hatching."

Dreams of Impressing a bronze were beyond Keevan's boldest reflections, although that goal dominated the thoughts of every other hopeful candidate. Green dragons were small and fast and more numerous. There was more prestige to Impressing a blue or a brown than a green. Being practical, Keevan seldom dreamed as high as a big fighting brown, like Canth, F'nor's fine fellow, the biggest brown on all Pern. But to fly a bronze? Bronzes were almost as big as the queen, and only they took the air when a queen flew at mating time. A bronze rider could aspire to become weyrleader! Well, Keevan would console himself, brown riders could aspire to become wingseconds, and that wasn't bad. He'd even settle for a green dragon: they were small, but so was he. No matter! He simply had to Impress a dragon his first time in the Hatching Ground. Then no one in the weyr would taunt him anymore for being so small.

"Shells," thought Keevan now, "but the sands are hot!"

"Impression time is imminent, candidates," the wingsecond was saying as everyone crowded respectfully close to him. "See the extent of the striations on this promising egg." The stretch marks *were* larger than yesterday.

Everyone leaned forward and nodded thoughtfully. That particular egg was the one Beterli had marked as his own, and no other candidate dared, on pain of being beaten by Beterli on the first opportunity, to approach it. The egg was marked by a large yellowish splotch in the shape of a dragon backwinging to land, talons outstretched to grasp rock. Everyone knew that bronze eggs bore distinctive markings. And naturally, Beterli, who'd been presented at eight Impressions already and was the biggest of the candidates, had chosen it.

"I'd say that the great opening day is almost upon us," the wingsecond went on, and then his face assumed a grave expression. "As we well know, there are only forty eggs and seventy-two candidates. Some of you may be disappointed on the great day. That doesn't necessarily mean you aren't dragonrider material, just that *the* dragon for you hasn't been shelled. You'll have other hatchings, and it's no disgrace to be left behind an Impression or two. Or more."

Keevan was positive that the wingsecond's eyes rested on Beterli, who'd been stood off at so many Impressions already. Keevan tried to squinch down so the wingsecond wouldn't notice him. Keevan had been reminded too often that he was eligible to be a candidate by one day only. He, of all the hopefuls, was most likely to be left standing on the great day. One more reason why he simply had to Impress at his first hatching.

"Now move about among the eggs," the wingsecond said. "Touch them. We don't know that it does any good, but it certainly doesn't do any harm."

Some of the boys laughed nervously, but everyone immediately began to circulate among the eggs. Beterli stepped up officiously to "his" egg, daring anyone to come near it. Keevan smiled, because he had already touched it . . . every inspection day . . . as the others were leaving the Hatching Ground, when no one could see him crouch and stroke it.

Keevan had an egg he concentrated on, too, one drawn slightly to the far side of the others. The shell bore a soft greenish blue tinge with a faint creamy swirl design. The consensus was that this egg contained a mere green, so Keevan was rarely bothered by rivals. He was somewhat perturbed then to see Beterli wandering over to him.

"I don't know why you're allowed in this Impression, Keevan. There are enough of us without a babe," Beterli said, shaking his head.

"I'm of age." Keevan kept his voice level, telling himself not to be bothered by mere words.

"Yah!" Beterli made a show of standing on his toe tips. "You can't even see over an egg; Hatching Day, you better get in front or the dragons won't see you at all. 'Course, you could get run down that way in the mad scramble. Oh, I forget, you can run fast, can't you?"

"You'd better make sure a dragon sees *you,* this time, Beterli," Keevan replied. "You're almost overage, aren't you?"

Beterli flushed and took a step forward, hand half-raised. Keevan stood his ground, but if Beterli advanced one more step, he would call the wingsecond. No one fought on the Hatching Ground. Surely Beterli knew that much.

Fortunately, at that moment the wingsecond called the boys together and led them from the Hatching Ground to start on evening chores.

There were "glows" to be replenished in the main kitchen caverns and sleeping cubicles, the major hallways, and the queen's apartment. Firestone sacks had to be filled against Thread attack, and black rock brought to the kitchen hearths. The boys fell to their chores, tantalized by the odors of roasting meat. The population of the weyr began to assemble for the evening meal, and the dragonriders came in from the Feeding Ground or their sweep checks.

It was the time of day Keevan liked best: once the chores were done, before dinner was served, a fellow could often get close to the dragonriders and listen to their talk. Tonight Keevan's father, K'last, was at the main dragonrider table. It puzzled Keevan how his father, a brown rider and a tall man, could *be* his father—because he, Keevan, was so small. It obviously never puzzled K'last when he deigned to notice his small son: "In a few more turns, you'll be as tall as I am—or taller!"

K'last was pouring Benden drink all around the table. The dragonriders were relaxing. There'd be no Thread attack for three more days, and they'd be in the mood to tell tall tales, better than Harper yarns, about impossible maneuvers they'd done a-dragonback. When Thread attack was closer, their talk would change to a discussion of tactics of evasion, of going *between*, how long to suspend there until the burning but fragile Thread would freeze and crack and fall harmlessly off dragon and man. They would dispute the exact moment to feed firestone to the dragon so he'd have the best flame ready to sear Thread midair and render it harmless to ground—and man—below. There was such a lot to know and understand about being a dragonrider that sometimes Keevan was overwhelmed. How would he ever be able to remember everything he ought to know at the right moment? He couldn't dare ask such a question; this would only have given additional weight to the notion that he was too young yet to be a dragonrider.

"Having older candidates makes good sense," L'vel was saying, as Keevan settled down near the table. "Why waste four to five years of a dragon's fighting prime until his rider grows up enough to stand the rigors?" L'vel had Impressed a blue of Ramoth's first clutch. Most of the candidates thought L'vel was marvelous because he spoke up in front of the older riders, who awed them. "That was well enough in the Interval when you didn't need to mount the full weyr complement to fight Thread. But not now. Not with more eligible candidates than ever. Let the babes wait."

"Any boy who is over twelve turns has the right to stand in the Hatching Ground," K'last replied, a slight smile on his face. He never argued or got angry. Keevan wished he were more like his father. And oh, how he wished he were a brown rider! "Only a dragon . . . each particular dragon . . . knows what he wants in a rider. We certainly can't tell. Time and again the theorists," and K'last's smile deepened as his eyes swept those at the table, "are surprised by dragon choice. *They* never seem to make mistakes, however."

"Now, K'last, just look at the roster this Impression. Seventy-two boys and only forty eggs. Drop off the twelve youngest, and there's still a good field for the hatchlings to choose from. Shells! There are a couple of weyrlings unable to see over a wher egg much less a dragon! And years before they can ride Thread."

"True enough, but the weyr is scarcely under fighting strength, and if the youngest Impress, they'll be old enough to fight when the oldest of our current dragons go *between* from senility."

"Half the weyrbred lads have already been through several Impressions," one of the bronze riders said then. "I'd say drop some of *them* off this time. Give the untried a chance."

"There's nothing wrong in presenting a clutch with as wide a choice as possible," said the weyrleader, who had joined the table with Lessa, the weyrwoman.

"Has there ever been a case," she said, smiling in her odd way at the riders, "where a hatchling didn't choose?"

Her suggestion was almost heretical and drew astonished gasps from everyone, including the boys.

F'lar laughed. "You say the most outrageous things, Lessa."

"Well, *has* there ever been a case where a dragon didn't choose?"

"Can't say as I recall one," K'last replied.

"Then we continue in this tradition," Lessa said firmly, as if that ended the matter.

But it didn't. The argument ranged from one table to the other all through dinner, with some favoring a weeding out of the candidates to the most likely, lopping off those who were very young or who had had multiple opportunities to Impress. All the candidates were in a swivet, though such a departure from tradition would be to the advantage of many. As the evening progressed, more riders were favoring eliminating the youngest and those who'd passed four or more Impressions unchosen. Keevan felt he could bear such a dictum if only Beterli was also eliminated. But this seemed less likely than that Keevan would be tuffed out, since the weyr's need was for fighting dragons and riders.

By the time the evening meal was over, no decision had been reached, although the weyrleader had promised to give the matter due consideration.

He might have slept on the problem, but few of the candidates did. Tempers were uncertain in the sleeping caverns next morning as the boys were routed out of their beds to carry water and black rock and cover the "glows." Mende had to call Keevan to order twice for clumsiness.

"Whatever is the matter with you, boy?" she demanded in exasperation when he tipped black rock short of the bin and sooted up the hearth.

"They're going to keep me from this Impression."

"What?" Mende stared at him. "Who?"

"You heard them talking at dinner last night. They're going to tuff the babes from the hatching."

Mende regarded him a moment longer before touching his arm gently. "There's lots of talk around a supper table, Keevan. And it cools as soon as the supper. I've heard the same nonsense before every hatching, but nothing is ever changed."

"There's always a first time," Keevan answered, copying one of her own phrases.

"That'll be enough of that, Keevan. Finish your job. If the clutch does hatch today, we'll need full rock bins for the feast, and you won't be around to do the filling. All my fosterlings make dragonriders."

"The first time?" Keevan was bold enough to ask as he scooted off with the rockbarrow.

Perhaps, Keevan thought later, if he hadn't been on that chore just when Beterli was also fetching black rock, things might have turned out differently. But he had dutifully trundled the barrow to the outdoor bunker for another load just as Beterli arrived on a similar errand.

"Heard the news, babe?" asked Beterli. He was grinning from ear to ear, and he put an unnecessary emphasis on the final insulting word.

"The eggs are cracking?" Keevan all but dropped the loaded shovel. Several anxieties flicked through his mind then; he was black with rock dust—would he have time to wash before donning the white tunic of candidacy? And if the eggs were hatching, why hadn't the candidates been recalled by the wingsecond?

"Naw! Guess again!" Beterli was much too pleased with himself.

With a sinking heart Keevan knew what the news must be, and he could only stare with intense desolation at the older boy.

"C'mon! Guess, babe!"

"I've no time for guessing games," Keevan managed

to say with indifference. He began to shovel black rock into his barrow as fast as he could.

"I said, 'guess'." Beterli grabbed the shovel.

"And I said I'd no time for guessing games."

Beterli wrenched the shovel from Keevan's hands. "Guess!"

"I'll have the shovel back, Beterli." Keevan straightened up, but he didn't come up to Beterli's bulky shoulder. From somewhere, other boys appeared, some with barrows, some mysteriously alerted to the prospect of a confrontation among their numbers.

"Babes don't give orders to candidates around here, babe!"

Someone sniggered and Keevan knew, incredibly, that he must've been dropped from the candidacy.

He yanked the shovel from Beterli's loosened grasp. Snarling, the older boy tried to regain possession, but Keevan clung with all his strength to the handle, dragged back and forth as the stronger boy jerked the shovel about.

With a sudden, unexpected movement, Beterli rammed the handle into Keevan's chest, knocking him over the barrow handles. Keevan felt a sharp, painful jab behind his left ear, an unbearable pain in his right shin, and then a painless nothingness.

Mende's angry voice roused him, and startled, he tried to throw back the covers, thinking he'd overslept. But he couldn't move, so firmly was he tucked into his bed. And then the constriction of a bandage on his head and the dull sickishness in his leg brought back recent occurrences.

"Hatching?" he cried.

"No, lovey," said Mende, and her voice was suddenly very kind, her hand cool and gentle on his forehead. "Though there's some as won't be at any hatching again." Her voice took on a stern edge.

Keevan looked beyond her to see the weyrwoman, who was frowning with irritation.

"Keevan, will you tell me what occurred at the black-rock bunker?" Lessa asked, but her voice wasn't angry.

He remembered Beterli now and the quarrel over the shovel and . . . what had Mende said about some not being at any hatching? Much as he hated Beterli, he couldn't bring himself to tattle on Beterli and force him out of candidacy.

"Come, lad," and a note of impatience crept into the weyrwoman's voice. "I merely want to know what happened from you, too. Mende said she sent you for black rock. Beterli—and every weyrling in the cavern—seems to have been on the same errand. What happened?"

"Beterli took the shovel. I hadn't finished with it."

"There's more than one shovel. What did he *say* to you?"

"He'd heard the news."

"What news?" The weyrwoman was suddenly amused.

"That . . . that . . . there'd been changes."

"Is that what he said?"

"Not exactly."

"What did he say? C'mon, lad. I've heard from everyone else, you know."

"He said for me to guess the news."

"And you fell for that old gag?" The weyrwoman's irritation returned.

"Consider all the talk last night at supper, Lessa," said Mende. "Of course the boy would think he'd been eliminated."

"In effect, he is, with a broken skull and leg." She touched his arm, a rare gesture of sympathy in her. "Be that as it may, Keevan, you'll have other Impressions. Beterli will not. There are certain rules that must be observed by all candidates, and his conduct proves him unacceptable to the weyr."

She smiled at Mende and then left.

"I'm still a candidate?" Keevan asked urgently.

"Well, you are and you aren't, lovey," his foster mother

said. "Is the numb weed working?" she asked, and when he nodded, she said, "You just rest. I'll bring you some nice broth."

At any other time in his life, Keevan would have relished such cosseting, but he lay there worrying. Beterli had been dismissed. Would the others think it was his fault? But everyone was there! Beterli provoked the fight. His worry increased, because although he heard excited comings and goings in the passageway, no one tweaked back the curtain across the sleeping alcove he shared with five other boys. Surely one of them would have to come in sometime. No, they were all avoiding him. And something else was wrong. Only he didn't know what.

Mende returned with broth and beachberry bread.

"Why doesn't anyone come see me, Mende? I haven't done anything wrong, have I? I didn't ask to have Beterli tuffed out."

Mende soothed him, saying everyone was busy with noontime chores and no one was mad at him. They were giving him a chance to rest in quiet. The numb weed made him drowsy, and her words were fair enough. He permitted his fears to dissipate. Until he heard the humming. It started low, too low to be heard. Rather he felt it in the broken shin bone and his sore head. And thought, at first, it was an effect of the numb weed. Then the hum grew, augmented by additional sources. Two things registered suddenly in Keevan's groggy mind: The only white candidate's robe still on the pegs in the chamber was his; and dragons hummed when a clutch was being laid or being hatched. Impression! And he was flat abed.

Bitter, bitter disappointment turned the warm broth sour in his belly. Even the small voice telling him that he'd have other opportunities failed to alleviate his crushing depression. *This* was the Impression that mattered! This was his chance to show *everyone* from Mende to K'last to L'vel and even the weyrleaders that he, Keevan, was worthy of being a dragonrider.

He twisted in bed, fighting against the tears that threatened to choke him. Dragonmen don't cry! Dragonmen learn to live with pain. . . .

Pain? The leg didn't actually pain him as he rolled about on his bedding. His head felt sort of stiff from the tightness of the bandage. He sat up, an effort in itself since the numb weed made exertion difficult. He touched the splinted leg, but the knee was unhampered. He had no feelin his bone, really. He swung himself carefully to the side of his bed and slowly stood. The room wanted to swim about him. He closed his eyes, which made the dizziness worse, and he had to clutch the bedpost.

Gingerly he took a step. The broken leg dragged. It hurt in spite of the numb weed, but what was pain to a dragonman?

No one had said he couldn't go to the Impression. "You are and you aren't," were Mende's exact words.

Clinging to the bedpost, he jerked off his bedshirt. Stretching his arm to the utmost, he jerked his white candidate's tunic from the peg. Jamming first one arm and then the other into the holes, he pulled it over his head. Too bad about the belt. He couldn't wait. He hobbled to the door, hung on to the curtain to steady himself. The weight on his leg was unwieldy. He'd not get very far without something to lean on. Down by the bathing pool was one of the long crook-necked poles used to retrieve clothes from the hot washing troughs. But it was down there, and he was on the level above. And there was no one nearby to come to his aid: everyone would be in the Hatching Ground right now, eagerly waiting for the first egg to crack.

The humming increased in volume and tempo, an urgency to which Keevan responded, knowing that his time was all too limited if he was to join the ranks of the hopeful boys standing about the cracking eggs. But if he hurried down the ramp, he'd fall flat on his face.

He could, of course, go flat on his rear end, the way crawling children did. He sat down, the jar sending a stab of pain through his leg and up to the wound on the back of his head. Gritting his teeth and blinking away the tears, Keevan scrabbled down the ramp. He had to wait a moment at the bottom to catch his breath. He got to one knee, the injured leg straight out in front of him. Somehow, he managed to push himself erect, though the room wanted to tip over his ears. It wasn't far to the crooked stick, but it seemed an age before he had it in his hand.

Then the humming stopped!

Keevan cried out and began to hobble frantically across the cavern, out to the bowl of the weyr. Never had the distance between the living caverns and the Hatching Ground seemed so great. Never had the weyr been so silent, breathless. As if the multitude of people and dragons watching the hatching held every breath in suspense. Not even the wind muttered down the steep sides of the bowl. The only sounds to break the stillness were Keevan's ragged breathing and the thump-thud of his stick on the hard-packed ground. Sometimes he had to hop twice on his good leg to maintain his balance. Twice he fell into the sand and had to pull himself up on the stick, his white tunic no longer spotless. Once he jarred himself so badly he couldn't get up immediately.

Then he heard the first exhalation of the crowd, the ooohs, the muted cheer, the susurrus of excited whispers. An egg had cracked, and the dragon had chosen his rider. Desperation increased Keevan's hobble. Would he never reach the arching mouth of the Hatching Ground?

Another cheer and an excited spate of applause spurred Keevan to greater effort. If he didn't get there in moments, there'd be no unpaired hatchling left. Then he was actually staggering into the Hatching Ground, the sands hot on his bare feet.

No one noticed his entrance or his halting progress. And Keevan could see nothing but the backs of the white-robed candidates, seventy of them ringing the area around the eggs. Then one side would surge forward or back and

there'd be a cheer. Another dragon had been Impressed. Suddenly a large gap appeared in the white human wall, and Keevan had his first sight of the eggs. There didn't seem to be *any* left uncracked, and he could see the lucky boys standing beside wobble-legged dragons. He could hear the unmistakable plaintive crooning of hatchlings and their squawks of protest as they'd fall awkwardly in the sand.

Suddenly he wished that he hadn't left his bed, that he'd stayed away from the Hatching Ground. Now everyone would see his ignominious failure. He scrambled now as desperately to reach the shadowy walls of the Hatching Ground as he had struggled to cross the bowl. He mustn't be seen.

He didn't notice, therefore, that the shifting group of boys remaining had begun to drift in his direction. The hard pace he had set himself and his cruel disappointment took their double toll of Keevan. He tripped and collapsed sobbing to the warm sands. He didn't see the consternation in the watching weyrfolk above the Hatching Ground, nor did he hear the excited whispers of speculation. He didn't know that the weyrleader and weyrwoman had dropped to the arena and were making their way toward the knot of boys slowly moving in the direction of the archway.

"Never seen anything like it," the weyrleader was saying. "Only thirty-nine riders chosen. And the bronze trying to leave the Hatching Ground without making Impression!"

"A case in point of what I said last night," the weyrwoman replied, "where a hatchling makes no choice because the right boy isn't there."

"There's only Beterli and K'last's young one missing. And there's a full wing of likely boys to choose from. . . ."

"None acceptable, apparently. Where is the creature going? He's not heading for the entrance after all. Oh, what have we there, in the shadows?"

Keevan heard with dismay the sound of voices nearing him. He tried to burrow into the sand. The mere thought of how he would be teased and taunted now was unbearable.

Don't worry! Please don't worry! The thought was urgent, but not his own.

Someone kicked sand over Keevan and butted roughly against him.

"Go away. Leave me alone!" he cried.

Why? was the injured-sounding question inserted into his mind. There was no voice, no tone, but the question was there, perfectly clear, in his head.

Incredulous, Keevan lifted his head and stared into the glowing jeweled eyes of a small bronze dragon. His wings were wet; the tips hung drooping to the sand. And he sagged in the middle on his unsteady legs, although he was making a great effort to keep erect.

Keevan dragged himself to his knees, oblivious to the pain of his leg. He wasn't even aware that he was ringed by the boys passed over, while thirty-one pairs of resentful eyes watched him Impress the dragon. The weyrleaders looked on, amused and surprised at the draconic choice, which could not be forced. Could not be questioned. Could not be changed.

Why? asked the dragon again. *Don't you like me?* His eyes whirled with anxiety, and his tone was so piteous that Keevan staggered forward and threw his arms around the dragon's neck, stroking his eye ridges, patting the damp, soft hide, opening the fragile-looking wings to dry them, and assuring the hatchling wordlessly over and over again that he was the most perfect, most beautiful, most beloved dragon in the entire weyr, in all the weyrs of Pern.

"What's his name, K'van?" asked Lessa, smiling warmly at the new dragonrider. K'van stared up at her for a long moment. Lessa would know as soon as he did. Lessa was the only person who could "receive" from all dragons, not only her own Ramoth. Then he gave her a radiant smile, recognizing the traditional shortening of his name that raised him forever to the rank of dragonrider.

My name is Heath, thought the dragon mildly and hiccuped in sudden urgency: *I'm hungry.*

"Dragons are born hungry," said Lessa, laughing. "F'lar, give the boy a hand. He can barely manage his own legs, much less a dragon's."

K'van remembered his stick and drew himself up. "We'll be just fine, thank you."

"You may be the smallest dragonrider ever, young K'van, but you're the bravest," said F'lar.

And Heath agreed! Pride and joy so leaped in both chests that K'van wondered if his heart would burst right out of his body. He looped an arm around Heath's neck and the pair—the smallest dragonboy, and the hatchling who wouldn't choose anybody else—walked out of the Hatching Ground together forever.

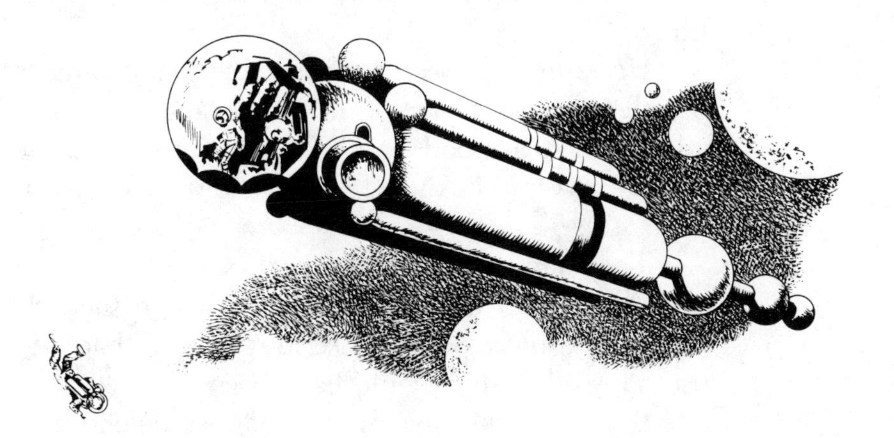

alone in space

by ARTHUR TOFTE

Arnie looked around at the bare interior of the empty ship . . . empty except for himself. Never had he felt so alone. . . .

It had been a week since his father had died. He tried not to think of it. At first he had refused to believe it. For a ten-year-old boy, it was a terrible thing to be alone on a ship rushing through space.

It had happened so suddenly. The ship had been hit by a meteorite. His father had gone out to check the damage. He had become entangled in the lifeline, which held him to the ship. In his struggle to free himself, he had opened a hole in his space suit. Almost instantly he was dead. Arnie had pulled him back into the ship, but it was too late.

Then it had taken Arnie a whole day to decide what to do. He knew he couldn't keep his father's body in the ship. Sadly, he had put the body into the air lock and had ejected it into space.

Up to the time of his father's death, everything had gone so well. Even being allowed to go on the trip had been a wonderful thing, coming as it did so soon after his mother's death.

His father had been furnished a ship especially designed to withstand the impact of meteorites and even small asteroids. Extra-strong pods had been built into the ship for their protection. Only in the open cabin did they have to wear space suits.

They had gone into the heart of the highly dangerous asteroid belt out toward Jupiter. Although their ship had been struck many times, no serious damage had been done to it. Any other ship would have been wrecked.

Best of all, they had actually landed on one of the largest of the asteroids. They had found a new mineral. Tested in the ship's nuclear-fusion power plant, it had proved to be extremely heat resistant. It was just what his father, Gregory Gambrill, one of Earth's leading mineralogists, was looking for.

With this material, it would be possible to develop better heat shields for ships entering the Earth's atmosphere. It could be used for heat bottles in nuclear-fusion plants. Heat-resisting metals had a thousand uses.

Arnie sighed in despair at how close his father had come to success. He looked over at the small canvas bag of samples of the new rock.

He had not forgotten what his father had said as they started on the return trip.

"These rock samples," he had said, "must be delivered to my company. If anything should happen to me, it will be your duty to see that they get there."

Then his father had warned him that the greatest danger on the return voyage would come as the ship passed the moon. There were space pirates on the moon who knew of the mission. They would try to get aboard if they could and get the samples.

Arnie had heard all about the so-called moon pirates—vicious men who preyed on unarmed spaceships.

Now, a week later, he knew from his father's timetable that he was already approaching the moon zone. His father had said the danger would probably last only an hour or so. He had also said he hoped they could zip through the danger zone without being noticed.

Then suddenly it happened!

The receiver in his headset crackled into action. There was a curt order: "Stand by for boarding!"

For a moment, Arnie was held motionless in terror. It could be just a regular Earth space patrol checking ships approaching the mother planet.

. . . or it could be the dreaded moon pirates!

Looking over at the bag of asteroid rocks, he knew he couldn't take a chance on having them stolen now. He had to try to hide them.

But where?

He knew there was no place to hide anything in the cabin. And there was no time to break into the pods.

As quickly as he could, he picked out one small sample. It would have to be enough for the tests they would want to make of it. Then he ejected the rest of the samples through the ship's waste-disposal vent.

He held the sample he had saved and studied it. For this his father had risked and then lost his life. Where to hide it? The very compactness of the cabin's interior made it all but impossible to find a good place.

He looked about frantically.

Then, as though his father's voice had directed him, he pushed himself through the airless space to where he kept his personal things. There he had the books and games he had brought with him. They were meant to keep him entertained on the long voyage.

Yes, there it was—his collection of one hundred Earth rocks and minerals. His father had given him the set to help him learn how to identify them. Each rock piece was held firmly in its own rubber pocket in the box. Each item was carefully labeled. Over the top of the box was a transparent plastic cover.

He felt a slight bump as the other ship began its coupling operation. He would have to hurry.

Carefully he slid back the cover. After a quick glance at the rocks, he selected a colorful piece of microcline. It would do as well as any. He put it in the right-front pocket of his space suit.

Then he slipped the asteroid rock into the hollow where the microcline had been. He slid the cover back on. Then he put the box back with his games and books.

It was the only thing he could think of. He hoped that among the Earth rocks, the one asteroid rock would not be noticed. At least he was trying his best to follow his father's wish.

Hardly had he put the box back into its place when the entry air-lock valve opened. Two space-suited men pushed their way in.

From the way they glanced around, it was apparent they were surprised to see only a ten-year old.

The headset intercom buzzed. "Where is your father?" one of the men asked gruffly.

"He's dead."

The men looked at each other. Then one of them turned to Arnie.

"Where are the rock samples your father was taking to Earth? Don't try to fool us. We know all about this mission of your father's. We need those samples."

"Are you the moon pirates?" Arnie asked fearfully.

From their expressions through their transparent helmets, the boy could see they were amused by his question.

The man who had spoken first grumbled, "We haven't any time to waste. Where are the rocks?"

Arnie gave his body a push and landed next to where he had put his personal things. He pulled out his rock collection.

"Here are my rocks," he said. "Is this what you want?

My father gave me this set before we left Earth. I know all their names now."

The leader of the two men came over next to Arnie. The man glared down at the collection.

Arnie was still talking as he pointed at one rock after another. "That's a wulfenite," he said. "And this is a chalcanthite. This is feldspar. This is a piece of coal. It really isn't mineral at all. And this is a piece of kimberlite. They find diamonds in this kind of rock."

The man grabbed up the box and ripped off the cover. His gloved hand raced along the rows of labeled items.

"These are just a lot of ordinary Earth rocks, just junk," he stated in disgust. With a sweep of his hand, he threw the box into the corner. In the gravity-free cabin, the hundred pieces went flying in all directions.

"Now you've done it," the second man exclaimed angrily. "How are we going to find the asteroid samples with all those Earth rocks flying around loose?"

"Search the boy," the first man ordered.

Arnie floated backward.

The man approached him. In his hand was a long, sharp-pointed knife.

"You had better tell us," he said. "If I cut your suit, you'll be dead in seconds. And we'll get the asteroid rocks anyway."

The man grabbed at Arnie. Without gravity, the two tumbled awkwardly around the cabin. Then both men combined to catch the struggling boy in one corner.

A moment later the piece of microcline was pulled out of Arnie's pocket.

"I've got it," the man cried. He held up the piece of worthless microcline for the other to see.

"That must be it, all right. Let's go, before the space patrol gets here. We've only got about twenty minutes."

He jerked a thumb at Arnie. "What will we do with the kid?"

The other laughed. "He called us the moon pirates.

What was it that the old-time pirates used to do—make their prisoners 'walk the plank'? Why don't we make him walk the plank?"

"Stop kidding around. We haven't time to waste. Let's just take him outside and give him a little push into space. That will take care of him."

The man reached out to grab Arnie. The boy squirmed away. The second man lunged to head him off.

Arnie found himself in a corner. Floating in front of his helmet were two or three of the rock samples from his collection. Almost without thinking, he seized one of them and hurled it with all his might at the pirate.

The rock hit the man's metal-and-plastic space helmet and bounced off harmlessly. But at once Arnie saw his advantage.

The rocks were sharp edged. If one of them tore even a small hole in the man's space suit, it would mean instant death.

The two men apparently realized it, too. One of them edged toward the exit valve.

"I'm getting out of here," he cried.

"Don't be stupid. Those rocks aren't sharp enough to cut into our suits."

He turned back toward the boy, who was cowering in the corner.

Arnie, by this time, had several more pieces of sharp rocks in his hands ready to hurl at the men. Before he could throw them, however, the first pirate was on top of him.

Here the boy's small size helped him. He gave himself a hard push that sent him under and around the angry man. Like a Ping-Pong ball on the loose, Arnie bounced himself back and forth, up and down, all around the cabin, using his arms and legs to keep the crazy motion going.

It was only a matter of minutes, however, before the two men had caught and clamped him tightly between their outstretched arms.

The pirate leader again pulled out his knife and reached for a better grip to hold the squirming boy. One thrust and it would be the end of the bouncing game. And the end of Arnie.

At that instant there was a slight thump to the ship. The men looked at each other in surprise. One cried out—"I knew we should have left when we had the chance."

Arnie slipped out of their grasp. He moved over to the air lock and opened the inner valve.

"Now," he said to the two pirates, "we'll see who has to walk the plank!"

"Not so fast," the pirate leader shouted over his intercom to the armed men of the space patrol who were crowding in. He still held the knife in his hand. He brought its point up against the boy's chest.

"Let us by," he said, "or the boy dies. He's our hostage to get out of here."

The officer in charge of the space patrol, obviously uncertain about what to do, motioned his men back.

Holding tightly to Arnie, with the knife pointed against the boy's space suit, the pirate leader started to push his way past the men of the patrol.

This, Arnie knew, was the critical moment. Safe in their own ship, the two pirates would kill him anyway. He had to do something himself . . . and he had to do it now.

He looked down at his hands. He was still holding several of the rock samples. One was a piece of granite.

Granite! And granite was hard!

He peered up at the pirate holding the knife against his chest. The man was staring back at the patrol officer.

Acting quickly, Arnie brought the piece of hard rock up against the knife. It grated along the edge, turning it upward and away.

The patrol officer saw immediately what was happening. He leaped toward the pirate leader.

Moments later, the two pirates, subdued after a short,

fierce struggle, were transferred to the patrol ship. A prize crew was put aboard the small but well-armed pirate ship. Finally, a patrol pilot was assigned to stay with Arnie until the ship landed. Before leaving, the patrol officer clapped Arnie on the shoulder and said they had been trying for months to capture the "moon pirates."

To the boy it all seemed like a bad dream. And yet here he was, still alive and safely on his way again. No "walking the plank" for him after all.

Alone again, except for the newly assigned patrol pilot, he looked about. The cabin was a mess. The pieces of rock from his collection were floating free. They were everywhere.

He grabbed at the empty collection box as it moved slowly by him. Then he began the task of catching each of the samples and slipping it back into its proper place.

He spoke aloud to himself as he captured the rock pieces one by one. He was still trembling from his battle with the pirates. But he felt his father would have been proud of how he had outwitted them.

It gave him pleasure to know and recognize each piece as he held it momentarily before putting it in the box.

"Ah, my beautiful malachite. And this blue azurite. And the brown limonite. And, oh, this beautiful piece of cinnabar. A piece of siderite, too. And this red rhodonite."

Suddenly he stopped. There, drifting slowly over his head was the asteroid sample he had saved from the pirates.

As he reached out and took it into his gauntleted hand, he knew what he wanted to do.

He knew it was only right that this new asteroid rock be named after his father. He would ask the people on Earth to call it the gambrillite.

the mysterious gem

by CLAIRE EDWIN STREET

"Hey, look out!" shouted Allen. A tall man ahead of him was jaywalking into the path of an approaching car. Allen was too far away to be heard, and the man kept on going. At the last second he jumped back, but it was too late. Tires smoked as the car crunched him to the pavement and screeched to a stop.

The man raised his head, looked around, and struggled to his feet. To Allen's surprise, he fled from the scene. He staggered badly, but managed to get around the corner. The man was not seen again. A crowd began to gather, and police sirens were heard in the distance.

Allen rubbed his jaw and looked at Kit. She was watching the scene intently.

"That's funny," Allen said. "What do you suppose he ran away for? He was hurt."

"It looked bad," replied Kit. "I think he was afraid of the police."

Allen stopped at the corner and examined the sidewalk as the crowd milled around.

"I thought I saw him drop something," he said. "Oh, there it is." A small red box was lying beside a trash basket.

"You're going to rub off the fingerprints," pointed out Kit, but she was too late. Allen had the box in his hand.

"It's a clue, anyway," he said. "I'm going to see what's in it."

He pulled up the lid. Allen and Kit gasped. A beautiful milky white gem was lying there, about the size and shape of a pigeon egg. Allen could see faint lines and dots in it. He tried to take it out, but it was mounted in the box and would not move.

"What is it?" asked Kit. "Isn't it beautiful!"

"It looks like a gem," replied Allen. He felt puzzled. "Only I thought they were put on necklaces or rings. Why is this one fastened in a box?"

"What'll we do with it?" asked Kit. "Do you suppose it was stolen?"

"It could be," said Allen. "Let's call my dad and then give it to the police." Allen's father was Dr. Jonathan Graden, a scientist in charge of the laboratories at the Star Electronics Research Corporation. He was a very practical man and would know what to do about the mysterious gem.

When Allen thought about this, the picture of his father's laboratory office entered his mind. Something seemed to grab him, and an orange light flashed. When he could see again, his eyes almost popped out. He was in his father's office. How could it be? He closed his eyes and opened them again. He was still in the office. "Where's Kit?" he thought. "How did I get here?" He was completely mystified.

Unfortunately, no one was in the office. He peered this way and that. He wobbled over to the window and looked out. He had somehow moved suddenly from the street to his father's office. He wondered what Kit had thought, seeing him disappear. Allen pictured her standing on the street, with a foolish expression on her face. As he pictured the street, something grabbed him. Again the orange light flashed, and he found himself on the street once more.

Kit rushed up to him and cried, "Wh . . . wh . . . what happened? I couldn't see you anywhere! You just disappeared!"

"I haven't figured it out," answered Allen. "I thought about dad's office, and suddenly I was there. And then I thought about the street and here I am. I . . . I don't know what it is."

"It's sure crazy," said Kit.

Allen thought for a moment and said, "Maybe it has something to do with this box. I can't think of anything else." His brain didn't seem to be working.

Just then a squad car slued to a stop in front of them, with a final wail of its siren.

Allen and Kit hesitated, wondering if they should show the gem to the police. Then Kit quickly grabbed the box out of Allen's hand and scooted around the corner and down an alley.

Allen quickly caught up with her and demanded, between puffs: "Hey, what's the big idea!"

"You got a chance to try this, and now it's my turn. Let's experiment with it a little and give it to your dad when he gets home. He'll know what to do. Come on, let's go to your house."

After reaching Allen's home at the edge of town, they tramped down to the basement.

Allen's projects were piled everywhere. He shoved the reflecting telescope he had made against the wall and stacked his shortwave radio, burglar alarm, and electronic organ model on the workbench. He picked up the mysterious red box and said, "I'm sure it's this gem. When I picture a certain place in my mind, something grabs me and takes me there. I'm going to try it again."

"I want to try it, too," said Kit.

"OK," said Allen. "But we'll have to be careful. We

don't know anything about it." He paused a moment. "See that lathe? I'm going to picture myself standing there."

Allen closed his eyes and pictured himself near the lathe. Immediately he felt the grabbing sensation and the flash of orange light. When he opened his eyes he had moved to the spot near the lathe.

"That's weird," said Kit. "Try it again."

"It's fun," replied Allen. "We could go anywhere in the world." He scratched his head. "I'm going to try it on something," he said.

Allen took a hammer from the workbench and laid it on the floor at his feet. He pictured the hammer lying on the other side of the room. He felt a peculiar pressure on the top of his head for a moment and saw a flash of yellow light. The hammer disappeared and reappeared just where he had pictured it.

"It works!!!" he cried. "It works! Now we can travel anywhere. Where do you want to go?"

Kit pondered as she stared at the gem. Finally, she turned to Allen and said, "I've always wanted to see the Eiffel Tower, in Paris. Do you suppose the gem will take us that far?"

"I don't know why not," said Allen. "Let's try it." He had never been to France either, but he had seen pictures of the Eiffel Tower, and he tried to picture it in his mind. Nothing happened, no matter how hard he tried. After several minutes had passed he said, "It isn't going to work. It's probably too far away."

"Oh, rats," said Kit. "Well, let's go to New York. I've never been there, have you?"

"No, but I've always wanted to," said Allen. "It shouldn't be too far away, either. I ought to have a picture of the place we're going to, though."

He dashed off and up the steps and was back in an instant with an encyclopedia. Kit turned through the pages, studied some pictures closely, and showed one of them to

Allen. "Here's a photo of Central Park," she said. "It would be a good place to arrive. It's pretty, and there aren't so many people there."

"OK, I'll try it," said Allen. He studied the picture and picked out a good place for them to arrive, off the sidewalks. He concentrated on that spot, but once again, nothing happened. He tried and tried.

"Doesn't it work?" asked Kit.

"Nope," said Allen. "I've concentrated as hard as I can, and nothing happens. What do you suppose is wrong?"

Kit was silent for a long time. "Let's try it again," she said at last. "Only, this time try to go someplace we've been before, so we don't have to use a picture."

"That's a good idea," said Allen. "It would be easier that way. Let's go to the Grand Canyon, then. You were there a year ago."

"Sure," said Kit, "I'll go first, then you won't drop over the edge." She pictured herself at one of the viewing points, and instantly, she was there. A few other people were nearby, but luckily, no one was looking in her direction. She pictured Allen standing beside her. Click. He was there.

"It worked this time," she said. "It's fun, but I guess we can only go to places that we've seen before."

"That's good enough for me," said Allen. "Let's go look at the canyon." They darted over to find the best view and gazed at the beautiful scene for a long time.

Allen grew restless after a while. "Are you ready to go, Kit?" he asked. "Where to this time?"

"What's the hurry?" asked Kit. "I could watch this view for hours. Anyway, this is enough. If we go anyplace, it better be your dad's office."

"Yeah, I guess you're right," said Allen. "This is too important. Toads! It's the best adventure we've ever had, and now we've got to let someone else take over."

Allen didn't want to leave right away, but after a few more minutes he became restless again. He took the gem, concentrated on his father's office, and started to send Kit there. He saw a brilliant red flash, and the rocks, cars, and people seemed to whirl round and round and round until they vanished in a blur. He couldn't see anything for a moment.

When his sight returned, he found himself standing in a strange room, with Kit beside him. Two creatures were facing them, while a third was working an odd machine. Allen couldn't make himself look closely at the creatures at first. He was afraid of what he would see. He stared at the machine instead. About the size of a portable typewriter, it had two wires poking up from the top, while a coil glowed greenly at the base between them. Three dials filled the front of the machine, and Allen tried to see how they were adjusted, though the figures meant nothing to him.

"Wh . . . what are they, Allen?" Kit asked. Allen tore his eyes from the machine and stared at the creatures standing in front of him. He froze, his stomach flopped, and his heart almost stopped beating. It was impossible! He had never seen anything like them. They had heads, bodies, arms, and legs and were dressed in blue uniforms, but there the human resemblance ended. He studied the being closest to him. The head was wider than it was high, with two huge yellow, unblinking eyes in a light violet face. Nothing resembling a nose or mouth was present, only a deep black pit in the center of the face slightly below eye level. Allen could see a movement of some kind of membrane in the pit. The head was bald but covered with tiny fingerlike projections about an inch high. They swayed to and fro in an ever-changing pattern which meant nothing to Allen. He began to shiver.

Allen felt he should say something, but his mouth was dry, and when he tried to speak, nothing came out. He tried again, "What . . . a . . . a . . . what are you?" His voice ended in a squeak.

The largest of the creatures turned his glowing eyes on

Allen. After a few moments he spoke. His voice had a nasal, squawky quality and tended to rise in volume and pitch toward the end of each word. "I am Paask," he said. "We are from long-off world which you know nothing, but we call Plax. We are pioneer scout. We travel to different world and explore. We are seek only knowledge and not harm."

Allen still could scarcely believe his eyes and found it hard to speak in his normal voice. Somehow he kept talking. "If that is the case, you can release us. We can help you. My father can bring many scientists to talk with you."

Paask answered sharply, "We are not being ready. We do not trust. We make known ourselves later. You need not to worry. For now we keep you locked up always."

Allen had a thousand questions as he began to recover from the shock. "How did you catch us?" he asked. "Did you use that machine?" He pointed at the machine he had examined earlier, but which was now turned off and no longer glowed.

"Yes," said Paask. "We did use teleporter. You used little one, and we could tune to big one."

Teleporter? Allen hadn't heard that word before. He thought it must mean a machine that can move things from one place to another without touching them. Then it struck him. The teleporter was turned off, and he still had the gem. He tried to concentrate on his father's office, hoping to send Kit at least. Nothing happened.

"Escape will not possible to you," said Paask. "We have nullifier turned on." Paask reached in his pocket and pulled out an object, which he held in his right hand. Allen couldn't make it out at first, but decided it was something like a pistol. It had a handle and a barrel made of several long wires held together by a delicate wire coil, which ran from the front to the rear of the barrel. Blue spheres, about two inches in diameter, were attached to each side of the base of the barrel, while a third, slightly larger sphere closed the rear end of the barrel. This sphere had nine small buttons on the back and, on top and bottom, two larger red buttons.

Paask pushed the top red button. Allen could hear a faint hum, and a bluish aura was given off by the coil along the barrel when Paask pushed three of the lower buttons. He pointed the pistol at the top of a chair, aiming carefully. A blue light flashed as he pushed the lower red button. The portion of the chair touched by the light slowly crumbled into a powder, while the rest of the chair was unhurt. Paask made further adjustments on the buttons and fired at the chair again. The area touched by the light turned black and began to smoke, almost ready to burst into flame.

Paask pointed the gun at Allen and said, "Anything I please I do with gun. You wisely at once give to me small teleporter."

Allen gulped. It was a most convincing demonstration, and he obviously had no choice. He placed the box with the gem on the table with the big teleporter. Paask put the red box in his own pocket. He then spoke to the other Plaxians with a whistly, squawky voice, accompanied by rapid movements of the projections on his head. The two other Plaxians herded Allen and Kit down a hallway in what looked like a very old, rambling house and locked Kit in one room and Allen in the adjoining room.

Allen examined his room, thoroughly dismayed at the sudden, disastrous turn of events. The room was lightly furnished, with a table, chair, and an ancient sofa, with several protruding springs. Everything was covered with dust.

Just then a key scraped in the door, and a Plaxian carried in a pitcher of water. He put it down without a word and left, locking the door behind him. Allen had a drink, then resumed his survey of the room. The window was barred and gave no chance of escape. It opened on a backyard bordered with trees, with a hill behind them, and gave no clues as to location, neighbors, or roads.

Allen knocked on the wall, and soon Kit knocked back, but the wall was too thick to permit conversation. He looked around further. The house, though ancient, had been somewhat modernized with electricity and central heating. A furnace register opened from the floor near a wall. A register? That would bear looking into. The duct was in the wall separating his room from Kit's. Before he could say anything a voice came through the register, clear and strong, "Hey, Allen! Can you hear me? We can talk to each other through the register."

"I can hear you," replied Allen. "I was just about to call you myself. Are you all right?"

"I'm OK," she said. "But what are we going to do. I don't like being a prisoner."

"We've got to escape," said Allen. "Only, I don't exactly know how. The window is barred, and we'd make too much noise if I tried to break the door down. You don't have a key, do you?"

"No," said Kit. "I don't have a thing. But these are real old locks. We might be able to pick them if we had something to work with."

"That's an idea," said Allen. "I'll look around and see if I can find anything. Hold on awhile."

Allen checked his pockets. Nothing. Was there anything in the room? He looked around but couldn't find a single thing that might work. He sat down on the sofa to rest and shot up in the air much faster than he had gone down. The spring was sharp! Spring? Hey! Maybe that was the answer. The wire was hard and stiff. Too stiff, if anything, he decided as he tried to break off a piece.

After working at it for a while, he managed to break off a piece about four inches long and get it more or less straightened with a hook at one end. He felt pleased and went to report to Kit. "Hey, Kit," he called. "I've got a piece of wire I think will work. I'm going to start picking the lock."

After a few moments she replied, "Good. I couldn't

find anything over here, so you'll have to get us out. But we probably better wait until dark."

"Well . . . yeah, I guess so," said Allen. "They might go to sleep at night, and they won't be able to see us so easily. Besides, they'll bring us some supper, won't they?"

"I sure hope so," said Kit. "I'm starved."

"Let's get some rest, if we're going to wait," said Allen. "It'll be a hard night."

Allen didn't get much rest, though. The sofa wasn't any good, and the springs kept sticking in his back. He dozed off once, but most of the time he waited impatiently for night to fall. The Plaxians didn't bring them anything to eat, and he didn't even hear them walking about. By the time it was dark, his stomach felt like it needed four hamburgers, French fries, and a shake. He waited for another hour, and by then a nearly full moon had relieved the total darkness.

Time to begin! Allen started to pick the lock. After five minutes he realized it wasn't going to be as easy as he had hoped. He kept at it, feeling different places in the keyhole and putting pressure on any projection, at the same time holding the door so that there wasn't too much pressure on the bolt of the lock.

He stopped and rested about six times and was beginning to get a little sleepy. At long last he felt something move. He increased the pressure, and click! the door was open. What a satisfying sound after so much work! He called Kit at once. "Kit!" he called in a low voice. "Are you awake?"

"Just barely," came the reply. "What's happening? Are you working on the door?"

"I just got mine open," said Allen. "Now I'll have to work on yours. I can't talk while I'm in the hall, but you'll be able to hear me working on the lock."

Allen left his door open to provide a trace of light in the hall and set to work on Kit's door. He thought he knew how to pick the lock after all he had done, but he had tc work from the opposite side, and it wasn't easy. However, he soon learned, and it only took him about fifteen minutes to open Kit's door.

Kit rushed out.

"I'm sure glad to see you," Allen whispered. "You're OK, aren't you?"

"I am not," she whispered in reply. "I could eat a whole cow, horns and tail and all."

Allen chuckled. "So could I. As soon as we get out of here we'll buy a dozen hamburgers. Let's go."

Allen shut the two doors and crept down the nearly pitch-dark hallway, with Kit close behind. He came to several doors, but they were all locked. He hoped to find one that was open and save the work of picking the lock. The house was big and rambling, and soon they came to a short hall leading off to the right. The room at the end was unlocked, and they entered with high hopes. A faint light filtered into the room through two dirty windows, and Allen tried to open both of them. Both were stuck, however, or nailed shut. Hard as he tried, he couldn't get a squeak from either of them. Meanwhile, Kit was exploring the room.

"It's no use," said Allen. "I can't get these windows open. No wonder they left the door unlocked."

"It's the kitchen, or used to be," said Kit. "I can't find any food now. Oh wow, how great a sandwich would be."

"Well, let's go," said Allen. "We're going to have to pick another lock, I'm afraid."

"Wait!" called Kit. "I've found something. It's a box of matches. We can see where we're going, even if we starve to death on the way."

They each took a handful of matches and returned to the main hall by matchlight. A big double door faced them at the intersection of the two halls, and Allen decided to try it. The room should have several windows. He set to work. It went more easily this time, and he took only five minutes to open the door.

They entered the room and closed the door. Kit struck

a match. Enormous Plaxian machines glimmered dimly on the far side of the room, green and blue monsters with coils, wires poking in odd directions, and a control panel filled with knobs, dials, buttons, and moving lights. Some old furniture remained on one side of the room, and a huge sofa lined the wall.

Allen and Kit were astonished at the size and complexity of the Plaxian machines, and several moments passed before they became aware of other ominous objects. "Hey, look at that," whispered Kit, pointing to a far corner of the room.

"Yes," said Allen. "I wonder what they want with that." He walked closer. "They've got all kinds of weapons. I see pistols, rifles, shotguns, and there's even a machine gun."

"Look at those pictures," said Kit. "They've got newspaper photos of practically every kind of weapon in the world." They had time to look at only a few newspaper and magazine photographs of cannons, tanks, warships, fighter planes, and bombers. Each picture was fastened to a piece of paper with writing on it. Allen had never seen such writing before and couldn't understand any of it.

"They're really interested in our weapons," said Allen. "Seekers of knowledge, are they? What kind of knowledge and for what purpose? It looks bad."

Bang! Something hit the door, followed by the rattle of keys. Allen felt his heart drop right down to his stomach. He froze for a moment before his wits came back and he said, "Behind the sofa. Quick!"

They dashed over to the sofa, pushed it out a little, and crawled behind it. They just had room to crouch down without being seen. The door opened, and someone flicked on a table lamp. Two of the Plaxians seemed to be scolding a third. Their speech had a lot of squawks and whistles, and Allen couldn't understand anything.

"I'll bet they're blaming that one thing for leaving the door unlocked," whispered Kit. Allen nodded.

The Plaxians sat down at chairs near their machines.

One of them turned on another lamp, but this one gave off a violet light. Allen could see their feet by looking under the sofa. The Plaxians were facing away from him, so he peeked around the side. They were watching a strange TV on one of the machines. Allen could see that the figure on the TV was a Plaxian and was talking to the creatures in the room. He seemed angry and spoke in a harsh voice. Paask and the other two were nervous and answered quietly. Once, Paask took several of the photos and held them up to a scanning device on the TV. This caused more chattering and whistling. At the end, the voice on the TV seemed less angry.

After a short silence Paask picked up a sheaf of papers and began reading them, occasionally showing something on the scanner. The reading and arguing went on and on. After about an hour they stopped, shut off the TV, and left the room. As Paask locked the door, he aimed more squawks at the one who had supposedly left it open.

"Whew! That was a narrow escape," said Kit. "I thought I'd croak."

"It sure was," agreed Allen. "But we learned something.

Did you see how they were talking about weapons so much."

"I sure did," replied Kit. "They must be planning an invasion."

"It does look like it," said Allen. "We'd better hurry and get out of here. I hope we can leave from this room. If I open the door again they'll know we were in here."

Allen tried to open a window. The first one was stuck, but the second opened slowly. It had no bars and was not far from the ground. Allen jumped down, followed by Kit. He knelt down, and she climbed on his shoulders and closed the window. Allen looked around for a way to escape, but they were inside a thick hedge which enclosed the yard. He couldn't see what lay beyond the hedge or how to get through it. He threw away the pick, in case they failed to escape. He could make another if he had to. They followed the hedge to the right and soon saw an opening a few yards farther on.

They were caught just before reaching the opening. Paask appeared in front of them, having used the teleporter. "Stop!" he squawked. "You no have chance. I shoot."

"Run!" shouted Allen. He darted to one side past Paask while Kit dashed past the other side. Allen pushed through the opening and found a country road. He heard shouting behind him and a lot of squawks and whistles. If he could only get out of sight. A large tree bordered the road a short distance farther on. He meant to hide behind it and get into a nearby field. Then he could go back for Kit if she hadn't escaped.

Paask suddenly appeared on the road in front of him. "Stop!" he shouted. "This is last chance." He was pointing the odd pistol at Allen.

Allen paid no attention. He dodged to one side and headed for the ditch beside the road. He saw a blue flash from Paask's gun and crashed to the ground. He seemed to be falling and falling. Then a cloud of blackness rolled over him.

It seemed ages later that he came to, but it could only have been a few minutes. He groaned. His head ached terribly, and he tried to rub it with his hand. He couldn't, and he realized he was being dragged along the ground. His captors pulled him through a door and down a hall to the room where he had been jailed before. Paask opened the door, and the others pushed Allen into the room. He was so weak that he slipped and bumped his head on the table.

"Get his key," ordered Paask. The two Plaxians jerked Allen to his feet, and one held him while the other searched his pockets. The searcher found nothing metallic.

"How you escape?" asked Paask, his enormous yellow eyes glowing.

"Find out for yourself," snapped Allen. Did the idiot really think he was going to confess all?

Paask stared at Allen for a long time. His huge, unblinking eyes sent tarantulas up Allen's spine. At last, Paask turned and glided from the room, followed by the other two Plaxians, who locked the door.

"Where's Kit?" thought Allen. Had she been caught, too? He stooped down to the register and called, "Pssst, Kit! Are you there? Are you OK?"

"Rats!" came a voice after a couple of minutes. "I hoped you'd escaped. I'm OK, but I can't stand those slimy monsters. They searched me for a key! It was disgusting. I'm going to get mad at them one of these days." After a moment she added, "How do you think they caught us?"

"They probably have a warning system outside," said Allen. "Then they just cut in ahead of us with the teleporter. It looks like we'll have to use the teleporter ourselves if we're going to escape."

"I'm afraid you're right," agreed Kit. "Maybe we can find out what room they keep it in. I'll watch through the keyhole tomorrow."

"That's a good idea," said Allen. "Let's try to get some sleep now." He left the register and stretched out on the sofa. "If I can," he added to himself. The springs were as sharp and uncomfortable as before.

Early the next morning the three Plaxians returned. Their violet, wriggly heads made Allen shudder. It was hard to get used to them, but his clamoring stomach brought his mind back to other matters. "When are you going to feed us?" he demanded.

"Later," said Paask. "It has not become time for eating. First have you many question to answer."

One of the Plaxians wheeled in a pushcart, loaded with machines and odd devices. They pushed the chair to the center of the room and strapped Allen to it. Paask set up two tripods, one on each side of Allen, each loaded with coils surrounding a long, thin cylinder which was pointed at Allen's head. A similar tripod was set up in front of him, only it had a maze of wires projecting from a central blue globe. Allen felt nervous just looking at it. What were they going to do to him?

Paask sat at the table, on which an elaborate control panel had been placed, and began fingering the switches, dials, and buttons. The side tripods came to life with a faint hum, and a bluish aura surrounded some of the coils. The globe in front of Allen threw a bright blue light into his face. Worst of all were strange feelings in his mind, as if someone were rummaging around inside his head.

Paask began to ask questions, harmless ones at first, such as his name, where he lived, how he spent his time, and so on. Allen answered them without hesitation, though it felt like something inside his mind was trying to force him to answer. The feeling became stronger, and Paask asked, "How you escape from room last night?"

Allen didn't answer, and the pressure inside of him grew and grew. Something was trying to make him tell about the pick he had made. He resisted the pressure and forced himself to say, "I threw away the key." It wasn't the truth, and he suddenly felt as if there were a fire inside his head. That machine punished lies! Could Paask tell when he told a lie? Apparently he could.

Paask said nothing, however. He continued the questioning, now on military matters. "Are any military base near your home?"

"Not very close," said Allen. It was partly true anyway, maybe twenty miles. He didn't feel the burning sensation.

"What kind?" asked Paask.

"Kind?" said Allen. "Why, it's air force, I guess." That was harmless information. Anyone could find it out.

"What kind plane?" continued Paask.

"I don't know, really. I've never been there," said Allen. But the pressure inside his head grew and grew until finally he was forced to answer, "It's mostly for fighter planes."

"How many?"

"I don't know, I tell you," said Allen. But the pressure grew and grew.

"How many?" repeated Paask.

Allen had to give some answer. "Five thousand," he said at last. If he had to answer, he didn't mean to make the figure too small. His brain suddenly felt like it was on fire, and it was all he could do to keep from crying out.

"It cannot so big," said Paask. He stared at Allen, his huge yellow eyes glowing. "You will more happy if tell truth."

"I haven't seen the place," said Allen. "How can I answer these questions when I don't know?" That was true enough.

Paask was quiet for several moments. "You visit base and come back," he said. "Then you can know."

"I won't do it," said Allen. "Anyway, why should I come back?"

"We have way of persuade," said Paask. "We have big reward. We put small teleporter relay under skin. We push button and you come automatic. Never fear. You fast come."

"I won't do it," said Allen.

Paask worked on the control panel, pushing buttons and turning knobs. Allen wondered what would happen next. This was a terrible machine. Suddenly, the room disappeared. He could see nothing, only a kind of gray cloud everywhere. He was still sitting in the chair. Without warning, the chair was gone, and he was falling, faster and faster, with the wind whistling past his face. Faster. It was a terrible feeling, and he felt he would give almost anything to get back to solid earth. A voice whispered in his ear, a whistly voice like Paask's. "I can save. Obey command and I bring back."

Allen thought fast. The voice meant he couldn't really

be falling. It had to be some kind of illusion created by the machine. "No," he said. "I won't help you."

The gray faded into black. Dots of light like stars appeared here and there. The speed of his fall increased. He felt he was headed toward a nearby heavy object, though he couldn't see it. Faster. Allen felt confident now, in spite of the realistic illusion. He could fight if it was all in his mind.

"It's no use," called Allen. "You can make me fall all day, and I still won't do what you say."

The speed of his fall began to decrease, and the gray clouds returned. Slower and slower. Finally he felt himself back on his chair. The clouds vanished, and he could see Paask once more.

"You are strong," said Paask. "You are more strong than portable interrogator. This afternoon we remove to scoutship."

"You're going to invade the earth, aren't you?" asked Allen. "That's why you want all this military information."

Allen was sure Paask's eyes changed color, from yellowish to green. His voice also seemed harsher and higher in pitch. "You will not to ask question. We advancing this sector of galaxy, but not to know plan or date."

Paask squawked at his two helpers, and they loaded the equipment on the pushcart and removed it. Then they removed some yellow strips of plastic from a sack. One of them wrapped a piece around Allen's left wrist and sprayed something on it from a bottle. The plastic stuck tightly to his wrist where it had been sprayed. Next, he sprayed the middle of the plastic strip and stuck it to the right side of the door. He fastened the other end of the strip to Allen's right wrist. The Plaxians left, locking the door behind them.

Allen felt the plastic strips. "What is this stuff?" he wondered. He pulled on a strip. It was solid. He jerked on it as hard as he could, but it held. It stretched a little, but it was beyond his strength to break or pull loose. At least the strips were long enough for him to reach the register communicating with Kit's room. "They've got us," thought Allen after pulling on the plastic strips about ten minutes. "I'm all worn out, and I haven't weakened it a bit."

A key turned in the door, and one of the Plaxians (Allen didn't think it was Paask) pushed in, carrying a plastic jug. "Here you stew," he said.

He turned to leave but Allen called out, "Hey, wait. Do we get to eat only once a day?"

"What wrong once?" asked the Plaxian. "We eat once, you eat once."

"We eat three times a day," said Allen.

"No three time," replied the Plaxian. "One time." He left, locking the door behind him. Allen could hear him unlocking Kit's door next.

Allen picked up the jug. It was full of a thick, brown, souplike liquid. He took a sip, choked, and spat it out. Whew!!! Did they call that food? He waited awhile, but he was so hungry that he tried again and managed to keep it down, but it didn't taste any better.

He called to Kit through the register as soon as the Plaxian had left her room. "Hey Kit. Are you there?"

"I'm here," she replied. "Have you tried your so-called stew? Wow!"

"It's nothing but slop," said Allen. "Fit for hogs, maybe."

"I doubt if they'd have it," said Kit. "I'm going to eat it anyway. It'll fill the vacuum in my stomach."

Allen groaned. "Yeccchh. But you're right, I guess. I think I'm glad we don't get such rotten stuff more than once a day."

Kit laughed. "Tell me that tomorrow. You may be glad to have your slop."

After talking awhile Allen tried to rest on the sofa, but it was as uncomfortable as ever. He got up and, after a lot of work, broke off one offending piece of spring and fashioned a new pick from it. He hid it under the sofa. He also finished the last of the stew, with an effort. At least it did give him some strength.

He was almost dozing when the Plaxians came for him. "Get up," said Paask. "You to answer more question."

They didn't have any machinery with them, and two of the Plaxians unfastened the plastic strips and marched Allen out the door, while Paask came behind, holding his odd gun in case Allen should attempt to escape. They marched to the end of the hall and through a door, which led to a stairway. The Plaxians herded Allen down the steps and into the basement. Boxes, lumber, and old furniture were heaped about helter-skelter, a rat's paradise. A path led through the rubble to another room. A tunnel opened out from one wall, running back as far as Allen could see, illuminated by glowing violet coils, which were fastened to the wall at intervals. The sides of the wall were hard and glassy, a reddish brown in color. Some strange force had been at work there, Allen thought. The Plaxians took him down the tunnel and after a hundred feet or so emerged into a huge cave, which was too smooth, glassy, and regular to have been natural.

But it was the occupant of the cave that took Allen's eye. "A spaceship!" he thought. Looming overhead, it squatted there, a sullen immensity as wide as it was high. A picture more of power than of beauty, it was shaped like a truncated cone, supported by three cylindrical legs. Too big for legs, thought Allen. Perhaps they were the propulsion system.

He didn't have much time to study the ship, for he was directed to the base, where steps led up to a door. The same violet lights illuminated the ship, which evidently had several levels, though Allen saw only one. A corridor divided the ship, with doors opening on each side. The corridor was narrow, and Allen marched down it with one Plaxian ahead of him and two behind. Some of the doors were open, and Allen got glimpses of large spaces crammed with machines, electronic devices, and peculiar objects, whose purpose he couldn't begin to fathom. Most of the rooms looked too crowded for regular use, while a few appeared to have been cleared, with the remaining machines neatly arranged. Allen thought the spaceship had originally been crammed with equipment, some of which had now been removed to the house. But why use a spaceship at all when they had a teleporter?

Allen had no time to consider the matter further. They turned into a room near the center of the ship. One side of the room was occupied by an enormous console, with dozens of controls, displays, and lights. Opposite it was a chair, bolted to the floor and surrounded by arrays of coils, lights, wires, and tubes. This was much worse than the installation they had set up in his room in the morning. Would he be able to resist them?

Paask perched on a chair at the control console and pushed buttons, moved switches and dials, and made many adjustments before he was satisfied. Allen could feel a pressure on his mind, and lights were shining in his face so brightly he could no longer see anything. Paask made a little speech to begin with. "I know you have small information. I need man to visit place and bring large information. We look different even in mask, and my speech make people to beware. Also your custom are hardly to understand. One of us hurt with car and you capture teleporter. Now we make you agent to bring large information. We treat very happy when you agree."

Allen could feel something in his mind pushing him to agree. He resisted and said, "No. I can't. You want me to become a traitor."

Paask's squawky voice became a little louder. "You have not choice. This interrogator have large power. No one ever resist long."

The pressure in Allen's mind suddenly increased. "How you escape from room?" asked Paask.

Allen felt as if a great flood were sweeping him along, compelling him to tell the truth. He struggled against it. His mouth almost opened to tell about the pick, but he regained control with a great effort. The pressure increased, and he had to say something or burst. He gritted his teeth and spoke. Once started, the words came in a rush. "I had a key, but I threw it away outside."

At once a knife seemed to cut through his mind, leaving a track of fire. It burned and slashed, the punishment for telling a lie. Allen suddenly became angry. Who were they to push him around like this? He wasn't going to become a traitor, no matter what they did. His mind was his own. He was going to keep it his own! His anger seemed to be fighting the cutting, burning sensation. The pressure built higher and higher. Just when he felt he could stand no more, a yellow light flashed, and the pressure was gone. The lights shining in his face faded away.

Paask growled something, and one of the Plaxians removed a small device from the console and replaced it with another. The lights came on, and a degree of pressure built up in his mind again, though the cutting sensation was gone. "You need not to think you win," said Paask, his voice shriller than before. "I see how you like Turpix."

The lights vanished in an instant, and Allen was left in total darkness. He swirled round and round, and the bonds holding him to the chair seemed to loosen and disappear. He was standing on a solid surface somewhere. Gradually, the light increased, and Allen could see that he was standing in a small plain surrounded by jagged, silvery rocks with a high, silvery hill behind them. The illumination was blue, and glancing around, Allen saw a blue sun in the sky. Where was he? There was nothing like this on the earth.

Grrruuunnnk! A harsh grunt, followed by the crash of falling rocks, sounded behind him. Allen turned, and his eyes bugged out. His breath caught, and he almost fainted. What kind of a monster was that?! A four-legged beast had stepped onto the plain. A long, narrow neck was topped by a large, round head, to which were attached four tentacles, writhing and twisting in all directions. No eyes or ears were visible, but a long, wide snout ended in an open slit with two rows of sharp teeth.

The creature extended its tentacles toward Allen and scurried heavily toward him. Allen turned to run, but the gravity was evidently stronger in this place, and it was an effort to move. It was like running in water—a lot of work and hardly any progress. Slowly, slowly, he struggled to flee from the nightmare behind him, but it moved much faster than he could. Allen redoubled his efforts, but before he could go more than a few steps he felt something cold and slimy slip around his waist and tighten. The tentacle pulled him around until he was facing the beast again, while the other tentacles held his arms and legs. He couldn't move an inch. The smell coming from the creature almost made him sick, but he felt much worse as it moved its mouth toward his neck, gnashing its teeth. "This is it," he thought.

At that moment he heard a voice, "Is not too late. You to agree to help and yet I save."

"Paask!" thought Allen. "Of course! I'm still in the room. This is just an illusion like the other time. I'm really still strapped to the chair." He flexed his right leg, and though he still saw the beast, he could also feel the strap and the chair. The scene with the beast became fainter as he concentrated on the chair, and the violet light shining in his face began to reappear. It went out suddenly, and the entire scene vanished. Paask was jabbing buttons on the console, which gave off an odd whistle. Finally, it stopped.

Paask stared at Allen a long time, his eyes turning yellowish green, then greener and greener and his scalp wriggling furiously. When he spoke, it was in a shrill, whistly voice. "You are to make angry. We finish to assemble interstellar teleporter tomorrow. I to bring real Turpix. Then we see you to fight. You will gladly to help."

He stopped as the other two Plaxians entered the room with Kit. Her eyes were wide, and she looked angry. One of the Plaxians removed the straps, and Allen stood up. As he did so, Kit broke free and ran to him.

"Allen," she cried."Are you OK? What's going to happen to me?"

Allen could see the Plaxians approaching, and he whispered in her ear, "They can't hurt you. It's just an illusion. It isn't real, and you can fight it."

He couldn't say more, for the Plaxians pulled them apart and strapped Kit in the chair while Paask kept Allen covered with his gun. Paask began his examination of Kit, and the other two Plaxians returned Allen to his room. On the way through the spaceship Allen noticed one room he hadn't seen before, apparently an infirmary. A Plaxian was lying on a piece of equipment. He was covered almost from head to toe with plastic, wires, and tubing. He was evidently the Plaxian who had been run over by the car.

Back in his room, the Plaxians reattached Allen's plastic strip to the door, then locked the door and left. Allen sat back on the best side of the sofa, too exhausted to move farther. What an ordeal! Would they try the monster on Kit?

Time passed. After what seemed ten ages he heard footsteps coming down the hall. Kit's door opened and after a few moments closed again, and the footsteps retreated. As soon as the Plaxians were gone, Allen bent over the register and called, "Kit, are you OK?"

"I am *not* OK," she cried. "I'm dirty and tired and hungry, and I've just been wrestling with an octopus. And now you ask me if I'm OK."

"I'm sorry, Kit," said Allen. "But I was worried about the machine."

Kit seemed somewhat mollified. "Yeah, I know, Allen.

I'm sorry. . . . Hey, they were angry when they couldn't make me do what they wanted. Your warning helped. I thought that thing was real at first, till I remembered what you said. Do you think they're going to feed us to a real Turpix tomorrow?"

"I don't know," replied Allen. "They could do almost anything, I suppose. I think we'd better try to escape tonight. I've got another pick made."

"How can we?" asked Kit. "I can't begin to break these plastic strips."

"I can't either," said Allen. "But we can try rubbing them against the table and things like that. Let's start as soon as it gets dark."

Later, Allen thought it safe to begin, and he struggled with the plastic without success for over an hour. He pulled, jerked, and bit it. He rubbed it against the sharp edge of the table for a long time without much result. "It's not going to work," he thought. He began to feel sad, almost hopeless. What was the use? What was going to happen next?

Then he had an idea. He still had some matches left in his pocket. The Plaxians evidently didn't know what they were, for the one who searched him hadn't paid any attention to them. Allen lit one and held the flame under one of the plastic strips. It gave only a little and didn't burn or break, but he thought it had weakened some.

He spoke to Kit a moment. "Hey Kit. Try burning the plastic with some of your matches, and then rub it. I think that will weaken it."

"It does weaken it," replied Kit. "I've been trying it, and I was about to call you."

"Good," said Allen. "Let's keep at it." He rubbed the burned place against the table and then felt it between his fingers. It was getting rough. He burned it again. He worked on it for a couple of hours. He burned and rubbed, burned and rubbed, until all his matches were used up. The plastic was getting thin on both strands.

He decided to take a chance. He pushed the table to one side and stood by the door where the plastic was fastened. He threw himself backward as hard as he could with his hands held out in front of him. Even though he was jerked to a stop, the left strand had broken. He tried it twice more, and the other strand broke. His shoulders ached from the shocks.

"Hey Kit," he called through the register. "I'm free now. I'm coming over to help you as soon as I can get these doors open."

"Fabulous!" cried Kit. "I'm almost free now, but my matches are gone."

It took time to get the doors unlocked, but Allen had had enough experience with the pick to know what he was doing. His own door took the longest, and Kit's came open almost at once. Good luck! Kit had one of the strands broken and was working on the other. She stepped on the strand just past the thin place and was pulling on the strip for all she was worth. Harder. Harder. The plastic gave way suddenly, and Kit straightened up with a snap.

"Uuggg!" she said. "I'll break my neck yet." She rubbed her neck a moment and said, "It sure feels good to be free. But I couldn't find out anything about the teleporter. I watched through the keyhole some, but I couldn't see anything."

"It was a slim chance," said Allen. "Let's go. We're going to find that teleporter even if I have to pick every lock in the place. We can't escape without one. If they catch us again, they might kill us on the spot."

"Better than being a banquet for an octopus," said Kit. They crept down the hall and off to the kitchen for more matches. They took the whole box and returned to the main hallway. The floor near one of the doors showed marks, as if something heavy had been moved in. Allen tried to pick the lock, but it didn't open easily. After several minutes of effort, it gave a squeak and opened.

"There's no teleporter," said Kit after looking around.

"No, I'm afraid not," agreed Allen. "Hey, what's that?" He lit a new match and looked behind a big, red machine. Pulling an object out, he peered at it with interest. It was one of the odd pistols used by the Plaxians.

"We can use this," he said. "I think maybe they brought it here for repair, but my dad can figure it out anyway."

Allen was picking the lock on the next door when a loud squeak disturbed the silence. It sounded like a roar to Allen. It was the doorknob of the room at the opposite end of the hall. The door started to open. Allen recovered and darted back to the room they had just left. He jerked the door open and pushed Kit in ahead of him. Someone turned on the hall light just after they had entered the room.

Allen left the door open a crack so that he could peek out. It was risky, but he thought they had to take risks if they were to escape. The Plaxians tramped up the hall, filling the air with their squawky speech.

Allen's heart began to beat faster and faster. One of them was carrying the typewriter-sized teleporter. Two of the Plaxians entered the communications center, while the other carried the teleporter down the hall toward the kitchen, and Allen lost sight of him. He heard the sound of a key scraping in a lock. A door opened and closed. Again the key scraped. The Plaxian hurried back into view and followed the others into the room. He no longer carried the teleporter.

"We're in luck," whispered Allen. "I saw one of them carry the teleporter toward the kitchen hall. Let's go."

Allen and Kit tiptoed down the hall. They felt exposed in the glare of the light, and in great danger. Allen was nervous as they approached the door to the communications room. One glance from the Plaxians, and they were finished. He could hear loud talk from the room as they crept along. The hall seemed endless.

Finally, after what seemed years, they reached the hall

to the kitchen. Allen checked the kitchen first, but the door was still open. Two other doors remained, one on each side of the hall. Allen whispered to Kit, "You try the one on the right and I'll try the left. Don't make any noise."

Allen gingerly turned the knob of his door. It seemed it would never stop. He pushed, but the door didn't move. It was locked. Kit's door opened, and Allen went in behind her. The room was empty, only a closet without any windows.

"We're in luck," whispered Allen. "Now we know the teleporter is in the other room. Let's pick the lock." He fiddled with the lock for a few minutes and said, "It's got a different kind of lock. I don't know how to open it. The pick doesn't even go in right." He worked at it for another five minutes. "I can't even start it. This must be a newer lock."

"Maybe we could break the door down," said Kit. "It doesn't look very strong."

Allen rubbed his jaw and after a moment said, "I think you're right. We don't have any choice. They may come out at any moment and might even take the teleporter away again. If I once get my hands on the thing, I think I know how to work it." He paused a moment. "We'll smash the door down together, and then you can threaten the Plaxians with the gun while I work on the teleporter."

Allen and Kit braced themselves and rushed the door. The crash echoed through the whole house. The door gave some but still held.

"Once more," shouted Allen, no longer trying to be quiet. They backed across the hall and charged again. Again a shattering crash, and the door caved in.

"Quick, take the pistol," called Allen. Kit grabbed it and pointed it at the door from which the Plaxians would have to come. Allen pushed inside the broken door to work on the teleporter.

The door to the communications center opened, and Paask stuck his head out. "Shut that door or I'll shoot!" shouted Kit. The door closed.

Allen worked quickly on the teleporter, but he had difficulty. He had three dials to adjust correctly, and he had not had much time to study the machine before. He put them in what he thought was the correct position, but when he concentrated, nothing happened. What was wrong? He turned the dials to slightly different positions and tried again. Still no result. He tried again and again. Had he missed something? He turned the machine on its side and checked the bottom for another switch or dial.

"Hurry, Allen," shouted Kit. "They're rushing me." The Plaxians had suddenly thrown open the door, and two of them rushed out, followed by Paask, who had a gun. He was taking no chances on getting shot himself, but he also had little opportunity to use his own gun. Kit pushed the buttons on the back of her pistol, but nothing happened.

"Hurry!" she called again.

Allen found something like a small button on the bottom of the teleporter. This had to be it! He pushed it and was rewarded by a faint hum. Two Plaxians poked their squirmy heads through the door. Kit had tackled Paask before he could use his gun and was trying to pin him to the floor. Allen had to do something about the nearer Plaxians first.

He clutched the teleporter and visualized them moving to the kitchen. They vanished, but he heard a crashing noise in the kitchen, followed by violent squawking. What happened? Had he made them bump into something?

He turned to help Kit. She was still fighting with Paask, who was about to get his gun hand free. Allen ran over and forced Paask's arm back. Paask was strong, but no match for the two of them. Allen banged the gun hand against the floor, and Paask's fingers loosened. The gun fell free, and Allen grabbed it. He stood up, aiming the gun at Paask, and backed toward the teleporter. As soon as he got there he visualized Paask in the closet across the hall. Paask vanished. He then visualized the other two Plaxians moving from the kitchen to the closet. The squawking noise shifted from the kitchen to the closet and became even louder. Maybe they had banged heads with Paask.

Now to get help. It was late at night, but Allen suspected his father would still be in his lab office. The plant was open day and night, and his father often worked late. But he would stay even later, now that Allen and Kit were missing. He would have to do something.

"Kit," he said. "We can't leave these Plaxians alone or they'll escape. I'm going to send you to my dad's office while I stand guard. Ask him to get two security guards and then stand in the room at the spot where you appeared. I'll try to bring you all back here. I'll give you say about ten minutes.

"OK," said Kit. "I'll sure be glad to get out of here." Allen pictured Kit standing in his father's office, and she disappeared. Allen waited ten minutes without incident, except that Paask poked his head out of the door once. The sight of the glowing pistol pointed at him was enough. Paask retreated and didn't show himself again.

After ten minutes Allen pictured Kit, his father, and two security guards standing in the hall in front of him. He had never tried so many at once before, and the flash of light was much brighter than usual. They all appeared, however. The guards were greatly astonished at first.

"Dad, am I glad to see you," said Allen. He felt weak all at once. "We've been kept prisoner here by men from a world called Plax." Allen told the whole story, what the Plaxians had been after and what he thought they meant to do to earth. He took his father to the open rooms and showed him the equipment while one guard watched the Plaxians. They also took him to the spaceship, and one guard was left to watch the injured Plaxian. After inspecting the spaceship, they returned to the house.

"What I don't understand," said Allen's father, "is why the Plaxians used a spaceship. If they have teleporters why didn't they just use them to send their team here?"

"I know! I know!" broke in Kit. "We tried to go to Paris and then to New York, but we couldn't. We had photos, too. You can't go anywhere you haven't been before because the teleporter uses the mind as well as electronics."

"Yes," said Allen, who wanted to add his part. "So they send out scoutships. They land on a planet and build a big teleporter that will work between the stars. Then they can bring a whole army if they want to, and I think that's what they would have done, too. Paask said they would have finished it by tomorrow."

"I think he was lying to frighten us," said Kit.

"Very likely," said Allen's father. "So now that we've captured the whole business, we've nipped this plot in the bud. They can't do anything without sending a new spaceship."

"Do you think they will?" asked Kit.

"We can get in touch with them before that," said Allen's father. "I'm not so sure they meant to invade us anyway. They may have considered us a danger and wanted to spy on us before making themselves known. We'll soon find out. Even if they are hostile, we have all this equipment, a spaceship, and I am sure there are computers and a library of books. We have nothing to worry about."

He paused. "Well, enough of this. It's high time you kids were getting home. We've all been worried sick about you. I'm going to work the teleporter this time."

He looked at Kit. She vanished.

"Wait," cried Allen. "I want to be in on everything."

His father smiled. "You will be. You can come back tomorrow." He stared at Allen.

Allen vanished.

the triple moons of deneb II

by DAVID H. CHARNEY

The three moons of Deneb II shone through the transparent dome, lighting the livestock compound with harsh triple shadows. The earth-type cows bawled in fright, huddling away from the dark shape that crouched at the entrance to their pen.

The creature moved forward slowly, belly close to the ground. The moonlight picked out reflections from the sharp claws; the naked canines were bared in a wrinkled-nose snarl. His eyes seemed, one moment, transparent, the next, like yellow lamps glowing from above the pointed muzzle. A triangular black pattern marked his fur, sweeping back from between his eyes to cover his sharp, black ears.

The cows, lowing in fear, pressed away from the inner side of the enclosure. They trampled each other in their efforts to get farther from the figure that crept toward them. The transparent glassteel dome offered an illusion of freedom to the frightened beasts.

Outside, the Deneb II landscape was a kaleidoscope of

jagged rock formations. The wild colors of day were reduced to harsh blacks and grays in the triple moonlight.

A calf, unable to compete for a space near the wall, turned in panic and ran awkwardly toward the gate.

A glare of teeth, a rasp of claws, and the calf fell to its knees. Blood poured from the severed carotid artery, making a black puddle on the ground. The predator stood, stiff-legged in front of his prey. The mad light slowly faded from his eyes as he lowered his head and lapped up the blood spreading around his clawed feet.

Tod Allen rolled over on his stomach, squeezing his eyes shut and brushing at the hand that shook his shoulder. "Mmffh," he mumbled.

"Come on, boy," his father said. "This is important. Get up."

"Oh, Dad," Tod said, opening one eye. "It can't be *that* important."

Dr. Allen didn't answer, and after a ten-second delay, Tod sat up, rubbing his eyes with the back of his hand. His light brown hair tumbled in every direction around his friendly, snub-nosed face. Once they were open, his amber-flecked, gray eyes looked with calm intelligence at his father.

Dr. Allen was the colony doctor, technical analyst, and chemist. He was still much taller than twelve-year-old Tod, even though the boy had shot up three inches that year.

The doctor was a thoughtful man. His prematurely gray hair and old-fashioned glasses made him look older than he was; an impression he was careful to foster.

"OK, Dad. What's up?"

"I have to ask you something important. Where was Rocket last night?"

"Gee, I dunno. I guess he was here with me." Tod looked around his small, chrome-and-white-plastic room. Rocket was a large German shepherd and till recently had been Tod's only playmate. The dog was asleep under the corner table, his rear end sticking out into the middle of the floor.

"Son, you've got to be sure. Last night, a wild animal killed one of the calves."

"But we don't have any wild animals in the colony." Tod shrugged in puzzlement.

"Exactly." Dr. Allen took off his glasses and polished them with his sleeve. "Our colony has twelve thousand people in ten glassteel domes. There are only four dogs on the entire planet, and ours is the only one in this dome."

"But Dad, he couldn't have done a thing like that. You know Rocket, he never hurt anything or anybody."

"I know, Tod, but an animal is an animal, and any of them can be unpredictable at times."

"How do you know it was a dog?" asked Tod.

"Well," Dr. Allen replaced his glasses. "There is some question about it. We know it wasn't a man. On Earth the signs would seem to point to a wolf, but there are none on Deneb II. It had to be a large dog."

"It couldn't have been Rocket. I just know that." Tod felt tears welling up deep in his chest. He held them back and forced his voice to firmness. "I'm sure," he said.

"I hope you're right. We'll have a council meeting tonight to discuss any steps we may want to take. Meanwhile, see that Rocket is chained at all times."

Dr. Allen ran his hand through Tod's hair and left.

"Rocket, come here, boy." Tod had washed and dressed quickly. Rocket just stretched out and yawned. Tod put his arm around the dog's neck. Next to his dad, he loved Rocket better than anything in the world. "It couldn't have been you," he said, but his voice was unsure. Tod put Rocket on a chain and walked him over to visit his friend, Stephan. He needed to discuss the situation with someone his own age.

Stephan Kracow had come in on the space transport from Earth only two weeks before. His father had replaced the original colony administrator. In a closed environment where few friends were available, it had been natural for Tod to try to become buddies with the new boy.

Stephan was thirteen, a year older than Tod. In spite of the age difference, Tod was taller than the slim Earth boy. Stephan's black hair was always neatly center-parted and slicked back. He had intense, black eyes and a pale complexion that accented his red lips. He always seemed quiet and withdrawn, watching the world from the corner of his eyes.

Tod tried very hard to be friendly, but it wasn't easy. Stephan often seemed lost and unhappy in the strange environment of the dome.

"Stephan, are you awake?"

Rocket was pulling at his lead and sniffing the ground near the door. A low, guttural growl rumbled deep in his throat. Tod tightened the lead, a worried frown on his face.

"What is it?" Stephan asked.

"It's me, Tod. Can I talk to you?"

"Wait a minute."

Tod heard Stephan moving around on the other side of the thin plastic door. Since the dome was weather-controlled, everyone lived in quarters made of the same lightweight material.

When Stephan finally opened up, Rocket went into a fit of rage. Stephan stepped back in alarm.

Tod chained the dog to a supply conduit and apologized to his friend. "I can't understand it," he said. "He's never been like this. I'm beginning to worry that maybe he *is* guilty."

Stephan stood silently in the doorway, looking fearfully at the chained dog.

"Steve, I've got to talk to you. I need your help."

Stephan stepped aside, and Tod followed him into the room. Like all the rooms in the colony, it had chairs, a table, bookcase, desk, chest, and bed, all made of the chrome and white plastic.

"How can I help you, Tod?" The pale boy's voice was strained.

Tod told him of the events of the night before; he ended the story saying, "This morning, I was sure it couldn't be Rocket, but he's been acting so strange I'm beginning to wonder."

"Yes," Stephan grimaced in distaste. "He scared me just now. He's a vicious dog, the only one in our dome. From what I've seen and what you've told me, it seems that your dog must be guilty."

"Steve, you wouldn't say that if you had known him longer. You've been here less than the full three moon cycle or you'd know he's always been much too gentle to ever kill anything."

"But there is no other explanation," Stephan said. He emphasized each word as though it were important to phrase the thought well. "No other explanation."

"I thought you were my friend." Tod was upset. "Rocket couldn't have done it."

"Excuse me, friend Tod, but I am not feeling well today. I am very tired. Perhaps we can discuss this later." Stephan did look sick, his skin even paler than usual.

Tod took the dog back to his own room. He sat and thought about the situation. There was no doubt that Rocket would have to be chained at night. The ecology of the dome made the death of a calf a disaster. It had been a senseless killing. The signs indicated an animal, and Rocket was the only animal in the dome. "No," Tod said to himself. "Rocket is innocent." Deep inside he felt a gnawing doubt; as Stephan had said, there was no other explanation.

There was only one way to clear the dog. Tod planned to lie in wait and catch the real killer red-handed. If some marauding beast from another dome raided the livestock again, Tod would spot him.

He sneaked out of his cubicle every night and tried to

stay awake watching the herd of cows, but it was no use. He found himself more tired every day. The tutor admonished him for falling asleep in class. Stephan seemed worried about him and tried to talk him out of his plan.

At the end of two weeks he gave up; he had accomplished nothing.

The last ten days of the lunar cycle passed uneventfully. Rocket was still chained every night, but the livestock incident became a thing of the past. Tod concentrated on his lessons, and even dour Stephan seemed more relaxed; they played chess every day after their classes. Stephan always won. He played a slow, thoughtful game, while Tod moved his men with great speed and dash. Tod would pace impatiently around the room while he waited for Stephan's move.

"Steve, what's this mean?" he asked, holding up an old-fashioned leather-bound book.

Stephan looked up from the chessboard. "Oh, it's just an old book that belonged to my grandfather back on Earth," he said with a strained smile.

"Hey, it really is old," said Tod as he opened the musty leather cover.

"Here, give me the book. It's a family antique and really none of your business." Stephan's expression was changing, the blood rushing into his pale face.

"Well, what's it mean? Lycanthropy?"

"It doesn't mean anything!" Stephan turned and looked out the window at the newly rising moons of Deneb II. His shoulders slumped, "I wish I had never heard of it," he said softly under his breath.

"Gee, Steve, what's the matter?"

"Nothing," he shouted. Stephan turned and swept the chessmen to the floor. "I'm tired of this silly game. Please leave now. Get out!" he raged.

Tod left in confusion.

The next morning, Dr. Allen was unusually quiet at breakfast. Tod knew something was coming. He finished his vitamin concentrate and asked, "Something wrong, Dad?"

"Yes, there is, Tod. It's happened again. Something killed one of our cows last night. Where was Rocket?"

"Dad, I had him chained to my bed. He couldn't have gotten out."

"Are you sure, son?"

"You know I wouldn't lie about a thing like that."

"I believe you, but we have to convince the council. They've asked me to bring you to a meeting this morning."

The council meeting was in the center of the dome. It was the largest room in the colony; there was a long U-shaped table, with the fourteen council members sitting in their places around it. Tod and Dr. Allen stood in the open area facing Mr. Kracow, the new dome administrator.

"Dr. Allen, we want to thank you for your cooperation in coming so quickly." The fourteen council members nodded in unison. "This is a serious charge. We feel that your son's dog has inflicted irreparable damage on our ecological balance. Our only recourse is to destroy him."

Tod stood with his heart sinking as he heard the sentence of doom. His mind wandered as he watched Mr. Kracow describing the charges. Stephan's father was a tall, cadaverous man with the same kind of pale skin and red lips as his son. Tod remembered hearing that back on Earth Mr. Kracow had been a count, a member of an ancient royal family in some small European country. He looked the part; his thin, straight nose was an exclamation point under the widow's peak that started low on his forehead, the hair lying straight back in two glossy wings. As he spoke, his expression was cold and forbidding.

Tod snapped back from his reverie in time to hear his father make an impassioned plea for Rocket's life.

" . . . the dog was solidly chained to my son's bed. It might have been possible for him to escape but not to come back and rechain himself."

"The boy might have found him and locked him up again," said one of the councilmen.

"No, I didn't," said Tod, his eyes filling with anger. "You've got to believe me. I didn't. Rocket was chained all night. You've got to give him a chance. There must be another answer."

The council asked Dr. Allen and Tod to wait outside. After a seemingly interminable half hour, they were called in again.

Mr. Kracow stood facing them. "Life in our colony is too precious to take lightly," he said solemnly. "The council has voted to give the dog another chance, but if there is a repetition of the incident, the dog will have to go. Two dead cattle in one month are already more than our colony can afford."

Tod ran to Stephan's room to tell him the good news. There was no answer when he knocked. Thinking that his friend was out, he went in to leave a message.

The room was a shambles—clothing torn, and strewn on the floor. Tod was surprised to see Stephan sleeping, curled in a tight ball, in one corner of his bed.

Quietly, he took a piece of paper and started to write a note. There was an old book lying face down on the table. Tod recognized the leather binding; it was the same book that had distressed Stephan before. "Lycanthropy?" Tod read the title and wondered what it meant. Why did it bother Stephan so when he had mentioned it? Idly he turned it over. The book was open to a diagram of the heavens, showing a full moon as seen from Earth.

Tod settled back in a chair and started reading.

Every few minutes he glanced at the unmoving body of his friend.

The book was an ancient one, more than three hundred years old. An aged, yellowed bookplate identified it as part of the library of Count Kracowicz of Transylvania.

Tod read descriptions of werewolves and discussions of the body changes that supposedly took place at the time of the full moon on Earth; the changes that could turn a man into a wolf. His eyes opened wider as he read on. Finally, he closed the book and tiptoed out. An idea was forming in the back of his mind. It seemed ridiculous, but he could think of no other explanation.

That afternoon, Stephan seemed listless and inattentive during his classes, and Tod took him aside after the lessons were over.

"What's the matter, Steve? Is something wrong?"

"Not at all, friend Tod. I am only a little tired. I did not sleep well last night."

"But you look sick. Can I help you?" Tod hesitated, then added, "In any way?"

"No, thank you. There is nothing you can do for me."

"My father is a doctor. Perhaps he can help if you give him a chance."

"There is nothing wrong. Just leave me alone." Stephan pulled away and walked off angrily.

The next three weeks were uneventful. Tod found Stephan increasingly uncommunicative. Tod's attempts at friendship were rebuffed.

As the three moons of Deneb II came into juxtaposition again, Tod prepared to test his new theory. He had tried to discuss it with his father, but Dr. Allen dismissed the whole idea as being too ridiculous to consider.

Tod watched Stephan closely. His schoolmate grew more and more restless as the triple full moon came closer.

Near the end of the lunar cycle, Tod insisted on speaking to his father. They were sitting at the dinner table.

"But Dad, I read it in his own book. More than three hundred years ago his family was cursed for something bad they did. I didn't understand that part, but since then, the oldest son turns into a werewolf at the full moon. Tonight we get a triple full moon. I think that even if this curse or disease or whatever didn't always work on Earth, here with three moons pulling at once, it's just too hard for him to resist."

"Tod, are you suggesting that your friend actually turns into a wolf?"

"No, Dad, I don't mean he changes physically. I know that's impossible. I think that maybe it's some kind of psychological thing and he goes a little crazy and thinks he's a wolf. That would be possible, wouldn't it?"

"Possible, but highly improbable."

"Well, maybe he needs help. He's a good kid in lots of ways. He says he's OK, but I think he's sick and afraid to ask for help. Maybe he didn't have this trouble on Earth, but now the pull of the three moons is too strong for him."

"Tod," his father said, "the whole idea is fantastic. I'm sure we'll find that it's one of the dogs from another dome that has figured out how to get through the tunnel barrier. The full moons are a coincidence. Forget it." His father finished his dinner with a caffeine pill and shook his head, smiling at Tod. "What an imagination," he said.

After lights out, Tod leashed up Rocket and slipped out of his room. The dome was lit by the triple moons. Distances were hard to judge in the moonlight, and even the most familiar things looked strange.

Tod walked quietly to a position opposite the livestock enclosure. He had prepared it the day before. A soft air mattress and a backrest were hidden in the deep shadow of an air-conditioning unit. He settled down; his chronometer said 2200, and he might have hours to wait. His stomach was jumpy, and his hands trembled with nervousness. It sure was scary sitting alone with only Rocket for company.

Tod put his arms around the dog for reassurance. Rocket curled up against his side. Tod could hear the peaceful lowing of the cattle on the other side of the gate.

The three moons hung directly overhead when Tod felt a low growl rumbling in Rocket's chest. "Shh," he cautioned the dog. His own eyes had been closing, but now they snapped open like released window shades. He held the dog's neck with one hand, feeling the hair bristling under his hand.

Something was moving across the way. He couldn't

see anything, but he was aware of the motion from the corner of his eye. He'd turn his head to try to catch it, but the harder he looked the less he saw. The confusion of shadows was an effective camouflage for whatever lurked there.

Rocket was pulling against his arm, and the low growl was becoming sharper. Tod couldn't hold the dog much longer.

There it was! A shape that flitted across a light area and disappeared into the blackness near the gate.

From where he sat, Tod couldn't be sure what it was. It looked like a large animal on its hind legs at the door; it disappeared inside. He heard the cattle bawling and thrashing around. Whatever it was, was in the enclosure. Tod felt cold sweat running down his back. What could he do now?

The beast was inside with the cattle. Tod was outside, alone . . . no, not alone, he had Rocket. The chain was being torn from his hand. Rocket was beyond obeying. His lips were drawn back, and vicious snarls rasped from his slavering mouth. If Tod was frightened, the beast had an opposite effect on the dog. Rocket was twisting and pulling at his chain trying to get at the thing in the pen.

Tod wanted to run and get help, but if he did, he was afraid the creature would get away, and this time, there would be no saving Rocket.

The gate swung open and Rocket pulled loose simultaneously. The dog threw himself in a mad fury at the thing in the door.

Tod stood frozen in place listening to the hideous snarls and screeches as the two beasts fought in the dark. He saw flashes of black fur as they rolled into the light, then disappeared into the multiple shadows.

Suddenly the fight was over. Whatever it was, it had escaped back into the pen. Rocket stood panting and snarling, his head hung between his forelegs.

Boy and dog guarded the door through a long night filled with fears and misgivings.

In the morning, when Dr. Allen and a group of colonists came looking for them, they were still in the same position, Rocket planted directly in front of the door, and Tod crouched against the wall behind him.

"Tod, are you all right? What happened?"

"It's in there, Dad," said Tod, shaking with nervous exhaustion. "Rocket trapped it inside. It's some kind of a big dog. I know my idea was crazy, but it looks like the wolf in the book."

The men, weapons at the ready, surrounded the door. Dr. Allen stepped forward and pushed it open. He stepped back in horror as Stephan Kracow, naked and bleeding from a dozen wounds, staggered out.

The thin, pale boy looked up at the men that towered over him. "Help me," he said. "Please, help me!"

the laughing lion

by RAYMOND F. JONES

The time egg lay on a hill near the castle ruins. Jimmy remembered the name of the castle: Winbury. Destroyed in A.D. 1354. They were going back to look at it before that time, when it was in its glory. It was supposed to have been one of the most colorful castles in England. But the way the egg was working, it looked as if their vacation would be over without their having seen anything.

Jimmy sat down on the grass and pondered the ruins of the castle. He thought back to when they were planning their trip. His father had mentioned that there had been a strange and mystifying occurrence in or near the castle the year before it had been destroyed. An event that had been passed down through local legends but had never been fully explained.

Jimmy's dad had shown him the passage in an old chronicle of the region. "In this yeare thair wast a verry strange and unnaturrall okurance. A verry visitation of tha devill or sundry daemons on the hill."

"Boy, it would sure be neat to find out what that devil or 'daemon' *was*," he thought, as he got up and wandered around the outside of the egg. Through the transparent walls he could see the repairman sweating in the cramped quarters to get the time-metering circuits working again. The circuits had quit last night, just as Jimmy's father, Mr. Madsen, was getting ready for a trial run.

The egg looked big from the outside, but with all its machinery, it was barely large enough to hold Jimmy, his parents, his two sisters, and his younger brother. Jimmy climbed the three landing steps to the inside. The repairman was on his back under the console of instruments that Jimmy's father used to run the time egg.

"Can you fix it so we can go on our vacation tomorrow?" Jimmy asked. He could see the upper left part of a very red, sweaty, and strained face.

"You'll be lucky to go by next Christmas," the repairman growled. "The factory never thinks about the guys that have to fix these things!" He wriggled out from under the console. "I've got to get some other tools from the truck. You better run along, kid. Your dad wouldn't like you playing around here."

"Oh, it's all right. I sit by him sometimes and pick the year we're going to visit."

"Well—just don't touch anything. It's all just the way I need it. Maybe you can go tomorrow."

"Gee, that will be great!"

Jimmy watched the grumpy repairman trudge down to his truck. The egg had to be parked on the hill. Here it would not interfere with anything in the last fifteen hundred years which they might cover in their trip. Jimmy was excited by time traveling. He climbed to the seat by the controls, where his father sat when they were on a trip. He remembered just how his father did it.

"Everybody—seat belts fastened!" Jimmy cried. "Door

closed!" He pushed the lever that would seal them in and start the air-conditioning system working if the power were on.

"Down time!" he cried.

He punched the red button that would set the machinery working and start the time egg on its preprogrammed journey. How he hoped the repairman could get things working so they could start in the morning to see Winbury Castle when lords and ladies lived there.

He climbed down and started for the door, almost flattening his face against it. The door had apparently closed when he pushed the door lever. It wasn't supposed to do that. The power wasn't on.

Jimmy climbed back on the seat and pressed the door lever in the opposite direction. Nothing happened. Everything in the egg must be broken, he thought. He felt like crying. They'd never be able to take their vacation trip.

He looked through the transparent walls to see if the repairman was coming back, but he couldn't even see the truck. He remembered right where it was. It *had* to be down there at the base of the hill. But it wasn't. There was only an old, rickety hayrack. The repairman must have driven off to get something from his shop in town.

Jimmy leaned against the wall to look out. He felt just a little frightened. He knew he shouldn't be inside the egg and wished he weren't. The scene outside was kind of fuzzy-looking, but it was that way sometimes when you looked through the wall at an angle. He shifted. It was still that way—just like when they were traveling down through time.

He listened and heard a faint whisper of sound. Then he cried out in fright. The machinery was humming. The power was on, after all. The repairman must have forgotten and left it on while he went for his tools.

Now Jimmy was alone in the time egg, and he was traveling to some past time in a machine that wasn't working right. For a moment he hid his face in his hands. Then he looked outside. It wouldn't do any good to get scared.

Maybe he'd end up in some year way back in the past and have to live there forever. With the time meter broken, he couldn't even tell what year he was in. Without the meter, there was no way back. He was lost.

The egg was moving through time slowly. The changing shades of night and day were like the flickering of a movie-camera shutter. The shifting seasons became apparent as snow and ice built up on the egg and then disappeared. The scene changed from green to brown to winter white, over and over again. He tried for a while to count the changes so he could know the number of years, but he lost count and gave it up. Exhausted and hungry, he at last lay down on the floor and fell asleep.

Then there was the sound of a familiar voice in his ears, and he awoke with a start. "Jimmy! Jimmy—can you hear me?"

He sat up with sudden joy. It was his father's voice. The whole thing had been a nightmare, after all! And today must be the day they were going on their trip. He'd have to hurry to get ready. But his hands struck the floor as he sat up. What was he doing in the egg?

He remembered then, and he looked outside. It was no dream. He was truly trapped in the time egg, moving to a point somewhere in the past. But he *had* heard his father's voice. He heard it again, "Jimmy, answer me—if you hear me!"

He understood. His father was calling on the time-shift radio circuit that connected the egg with the central control headquarters whenever they were on a trip. It was always connected to the power system of the egg when the door was locked and sealed. And he knew now why he couldn't open the door when he tried. It would never open while the egg was traveling.

"Dad! I hear you!" Jimmy cried. "I hear you—"

He heard his father sigh in exhausted relief. "Thank heavens. What happened, Jimmy?"

Jimmy explained quickly what he had done. He heard his father speak roughly to someone, and Jimmy guessed it must be the repairman who had left the power on when he left the ship.

"It's all my fault," Jimmy said. "Can you tell me how to get the ship back? If you'll tell me exactly what to do, I'll do just what you say, so I can come home."

"I'm afraid it isn't that easy, son. We're working hard on it, but the damaged time-meter circuits won't let the ship operate normally. We'll get you back as quickly as we can. We'll have to do it from this end, but we can't do it until we know exactly what time you're in. Is the egg still moving?"

Jimmy looked outside. The days and nights were now moving slowly by. He described it to his father.

"Tell me what you see outside," said Mr. Madsen. "What does the castle look like?"

"It's all built up," said Jimmy. "It's not a ruin anymore."

"Are there people going in and out of it?"

"Yes. Lots of them. I see them every now and then."

Jimmy heard the whisper of conversation between his father and some other men in the control room. "He's earlier than 1354," said Mr. Madsen. "Winbury was destroyed that year. He seems to be stopping somewhere in the last years of Winbury's history, I'd say."

Jimmy stared at the scene outside. "I'm slowing down!" he exclaimed. "It's going to stop in a minute!"

"Good. Tell me exactly when you think you are stopped. You can tell if you see someone walking. His movements will appear normal."

"There! I'm stopped. A whole bunch of people are going in and out of the castle across the moat. And there are some people in a field right below me. They're cutting grain. Now one of them has seen me, and he's coming for me!"

The man running up the hill was a bearded, rough-looking character, wearing baggy pants and a loose shirt that looked as if they had not been washed for years. He carried a large stick. Two other men followed. In a moment, all three were standing just outside the egg, gesturing in wild excitement.

"Turn on the outside microphone," said Mr. Madsen. "We want to hear what they are saying."

Jimmy did so, but he could scarcely understand a word, even though it was English the men spoke. Suddenly, the first man approached the egg boldly and brought his stick down in a smashing blow. Then he ran.

"Stop that!" Jimmy cried. "You'll break the egg!"

"What are they doing?" asked Mr. Madsen.

"They hit the egg with a stick. But they ran away."

"I hope there's nothing more like that. The shell could fracture."

It was evening and growing dark rapidly. In the twilight, Jimmy could see that many people were gathered in the distance, pointing in his direction. He could tell they were both frightened and excited. But no one else came near as night came on. The helpless egg lay alone in the night.

Jimmy's father told him to try to get some sleep, and even though he was starved and thirsty, he did so easily. He awoke at daybreak. The sky was bleak. It was raining. And on the ground were some platters and packages placed there during the night.

Food!

He touched the door lever, then stopped and told his father what he had found. "Don't touch that food," said Mr. Madsen. "You'd be very sick if you ate any of it. Sanitation doesn't exist in your time. Your stomach couldn't stand the filth and germs in those dishes. But if it's raining, open the door and catch some rainwater to drink. Look in the food cabinet. I think there's a deep bowl in the box of picnic things. Can you see it?"

"I've got it."

"Be careful. If anybody comes within half a mile, lock up."

Jimmy caught enough water to ease his thirst and to save a little. At midmorning the sky began to clear. Then Jimmy saw some more people coming from the castle.

"There's a man on a white horse," Jimmy told his father. "He's dressed like a knight. He's got chain mail and a helmet with an open visor. About a dozen other knights are with him. And a lot of others, who aren't in armor."

"That must be the lord of the castle," said Mr. Madsen. "If we only knew who he is, we could pinpoint the time you're in. Tell us more about the people and what they look like."

"Just like knights in chain-mail armor," said Jimmy. He described more detail as the group approached, but nothing seemed to help his father and the other men at the control center.

"I'm hungry," said Jimmy. "Can't you hurry, Dad?"

"A lot of people are working hard to get you back, Jimmy. Try to be patient a little longer. Tell me what the people are doing."

"The knights are riding around the egg, just looking it over. They're stopping and talking to each other. It looks like the main knight has ordered the other people to do something. Some of them are riding off, and he's waiting," Jimmy answered.

For an hour more, nothing happened, and then Jimmy saw them coming out of the castle with some kind of carriage drawn by horses. It looked like a square, open platform made of beams, with wheels attached. "They're bringing it up to me. What do you suppose they are going to do?" asked Jimmy.

"I can't imagine—"

Minutes later, Jimmy understood. "Dad! They're taking the beams apart and bringing them alongside the egg. They're going to pick up the egg and they're going to take me into the castle!"

There was a babble of unhappy conversation at the other end. Jimmy knew that moving the egg would upset the location factors and probably put him into the same space that other objects would occupy at some time during the trip back to his own time. The egg and Jimmy would be destroyed if this should happen.

There was some kind of commotion near the castle, and a man on a gray horse came riding swiftly in the direction of those gathered about the egg. As the rider came close, Jimmy saw that he was a thin-faced old man with a hawkish nose. He had a brown robe with a cowl that hung at the back of his head. A monk, Jimmy guessed. He told his father.

"Watch. See what he's up to," said Mr. Madsen.

The monk approached the main knight insolently, screaming and yelling and waving his hands at him. The knight reined in his horse and almost brought its prancing hooves down on the head of the furious monk.

"I can't understand them," said Jimmy. "Can you tell me what they're arguing about, Dad?"

"The monk doesn't want the egg brought into the castle. He says it's something sent by the Devil and that a curse will come upon the whole castle if they bring it in."

"What does he want them to do?"

There was a long pause and silence on the other end. Finally, Mr. Madsen spoke. "He wants them to place fagots around the egg and destroy it by fire."

"Dad!"

"Listen, son. We'll try to get you back home before they can harm you. But if we can't, we'll move you to another period and work from there. We've almost plotted a line to you, and we'll have to start all over again if we're forced to move you. We know you're tired and you've been

without food for a long time, Jimmy. But we've got a dozen of the best time experts in the world here working on the problem. We'll get you out, Jimmy."

"Yeah, sure, Dad."

Jimmy felt now for the first time that maybe they wouldn't get him out. His father was speaking bravely, but they really didn't know how to bring him back, he thought.

A furious argument raged between the monk and the knight. Finally, the knight gave a signal, and the beams were moved away and carried back to the castle. And then Jimmy's heart froze. Coming across the moat were load after load of small fagots and other firewood.

"They're going to start piling wood up around the

egg," Jimmy said. "They're going to burn it. The egg won't stand it, will it?"

"No," said Mr. Madsen. "It would destroy the egg and you, too. We'll have to pull you out to another time, then start our work all over again."

It wouldn't work, Jimmy thought. If they had to move him, he'd be completely lost.

"Tell us everything that's happening, Jimmy," said Mr. Madsen.

Jimmy felt too discouraged to say much. Finally, he said, "They're piling up the wood. It's so high now I can't see over it except by standing up on your control chair. The monk is flapping his hands around and laughing like crazy. How can he be such a mean man?"

"There are good ones and mean ones in every age."

"The other people don't look too happy. The knight looks the unhappiest of all. He's taken off his helmet. I like him. He wouldn't do this, but he's scared of the monk. If I could talk to him, maybe I could convince him I'm not going to hurt anybody. Maybe he'd let me live here. If you'd let me try to open the door, I might be able to push the wood away and get to him even now."

"You might never get back inside the egg."

"Maybe I could stay alive here. If they burn the egg—"

"We'll move you before that happens."

"The knight is riding around. He looks like he's almost ready to tell the monk it's all off, but I guess he doesn't dare. He looks like a real brave man, though. I guess he's just superstitious. He's got a picture on the shirt that goes over his coat of mail. It looks like a lion standing on its hind legs with its paws in the air ready to fight. But it knows it can win. It's laughing. Just like I'll bet the knight does when he goes into battle. I'll bet he goes laughing."

There was a sudden burst from the radio. Jimmy's father cried out, "The Laughing Lion! Now we know who the knight is! He's David of Winbury. David Winbury—he occupied the castle only a single year before he was killed in the battle that left the place in ruins. Jimmy, what does the season look like? What time of year? Summer, fall, spring—can you tell?"

"It looks like about the end of summer. Trees are a little yellow, and people are harvesting in the fields like I told you."

"August—in the year 1353! It's got to be within days of the right time. Jimmy—it'll be only a few minutes now, and we'll have the equations worked out to set the controls for your return. Just a few minutes, Jimmy—"

There wouldn't be a few minutes. Jimmy saw a sudden flash of yellow, flickering in the spaces through the fagots. "Dad! They've set fire to the wood. It's beginning to burn all around the egg!"

"A minute more, Jimmy—a minute more!" His father's voice was desperate.

But the time was gone. It was too late, Jimmy thought. The heat was beginning to penetrate the walls of the egg. Suddenly a sharp report, like the crack of a rifle, burst upon Jimmy's ears. He looked up. A two-foot crack appeared above his head in the plastic wall of the egg.

He could hear the urgent, frantic conversation on the

radio among his father and the technicians as they struggled to obtain the equations from the computers and set them into the controls. It was no use telling them of the crack. It would only delay them more. And it didn't matter. It really didn't matter at all now—

He felt dizzy and sick with the suffocating heat that was pouring upon him. The air within the egg was like a furnace blast. The fagots had burned down a little, and he could see the crowd outside watching grimly.

Suddenly, there was a violent movement among the people. A horseman was riding furiously. The knight. The Laughing Lion. He was riding toward the egg, his visor lowered. In his hand was a lance he had taken from one of the other knights. The lance was lowered and aimed directly at the egg.

Jimmy cried out. He couldn't believe it. The Laughing Lion had tried to protect him. But now the lance was driving like an arrow toward him, propelled by the pounding hooves of the great stallion on which the knight rode.

One thrust of that lance would shatter the damaged egg like a bowl of glass.

Jimmy watched, fearful and unbelieving, his hands and face pressed against the hot wall of the egg.

The horse and rider and the shattering lance were upon him. But the lance didn't strike the egg. It struck the burning fagots and scattered them in a flaming shower over the landscape.

The rider turned. He came back, lance lowered, and scattered the burning brands on the other side of the egg. The fire died away, and the air within the egg began to cool.

Once again, the Laughing Lion approached. More slowly now. The knight raised his visor, lifted the lance upright, and rested it in its socket. He rode slowly by, a smile on his face as he saluted the boy.

Jimmy waved back. "Thank you!" he shouted. In the background the raging monk shrieked and tore his robe.

Jimmy's father cried out over the radio. "We've got it, Jimmy! Are you all right?"

"Yes—yes, Dad. I'm all right. What do you want me to do?"

"Press the return button, Jimmy. Press it quickly!"

The knight was still smiling at him as Jimmy climbed up on the control seat and pressed the button.

As Jimmy stumbled out the door of the time egg, he heard sobbing and laughing. The egg was still on the hill, but in his own time. His father and his mother were there, and his brother and sisters. A whole crowd of other people he didn't know were there, too.

His father hugged him fiercely. "If only you'd told us about the Laughing Lion when you first saw him," said Mr. Madsen.

"I didn't think. I didn't know it was important."

"Of course you didn't. You couldn't have known."

"Can we start our vacation tomorrow?"

His father laughed. "I should think you'd have seen enough of time traveling for a while."

"No, sir! And do you know what I want to do?"

"What, Jimmy?"

"I want to go back and thank the man—Sir David Winbury. The Laughing Lion. He never did want to hurt me. It was just that crazy old monk. The Laughing Lion was a nice man. He saved my life."

Mr. Madsen nodded his assent, and Jimmy added, "You know what else? I found out about that strange occurrence on the hill, too. That was no devil or demon—that was *me!*"

two years to gaea

by NICK BOLES

I was scared . . . my heart pounding . . . unable to take my eyes away from the madman facing me.

I am only twelve years old. But I had seen enough madness in the past few months to recognize it.

Now I was seeing it again . . . madness that so far had brought death with it every time it came. I knew I shouldn't panic . . . and yet his blazing eyes were fixed on me . . . and I had no place to run away from him.

One by one the five members of the crew of the spaceship *Hermes VI* had gone mad. Two long years confined in the tiny cabin had been too much for them. Each, in his madness, had become a threat to the others. Lacking any means to treat them or control them, Captain Turner had pushed them out through the exhaust vent.

Now only Captain Turner and I were left. And now he, too, had gone mad—just a few hours before we were to reach our destination, the planet Gaea.

As he stood opposite me, all I could see were the crazed

look in his eyes and the way his hands were moving convulsively, as though he had no control over them.

I tried to keep from showing the terrible fear that gripped me. My hands shook. My legs seemed made of rubber under me.

Always Captain Turner had been the strong one, the steady one. As the crew members had slipped out of sanity, it had been his strength that had kept us alive. He had fought with them in their violence. And it had been his strong hands that had pushed their still-living bodies out into the cold, empty space.

Those hands were now reaching out for me.

I pressed back against the cabin wall in an effort to escape those powerful, clutching hands.

I tried probing his mind. It was no use. His mind was a whirlpool of maniacal disorder and confusion. There simply was no reason there, nothing to touch with my own mind.

I had no weapons. Even if I had, I wondered if I could have used them on Captain Turner. Through the long two years of our voyage, he had been like a father to me—far more than my own real father had been to me back on Earth. My own father had always despised me because of my telepathic powers, which could read his mind. He always called me his "freak" son, for my strange powers and other reasons, too.

Perhaps I was a freak. And yet it was the reason I was on the *Hermes VI*. I was brought along on the survey trip to Gaea because of my telepathic ability. I could read people's minds. It didn't matter what language they used, I could "receive" their thoughts and translate them into my own language.

Gaea had been discovered by a two-man exploration team. Captain Turner had told me they named the planet after a prehistoric Greek earth-goddess. They had reported back that the planet's climate and atmosphere were ideal for human life. Just as important, they stated that it was rich in all the natural resources so desperately needed by humans.

It was to be my task when we reached Gaea to "communicate" with the humanoid natives, which the original explorers had observed but never actually contacted.

If only I could now reach the captain's mind and communicate with him, I might be able to calm him down. But, hard as I tried, all I could receive from him was a tangled blur of frenzied rage. The others, when they went mad, had been overcome by the captain. Now it was the captain who was mad.

I tried talking to him, my voice dry and rasping.

"Captain Turner," I cried out. "Get hold of yourself! We are almost to Gaea—another few hours."

He shook his head in nonunderstanding.

I tried another tack.

"You must be hungry," I said. "Let me get you something to eat."

For a moment sanity seemed to come into his expression. He rubbed his eyes and again shook his head as though to dispel the fog that filled him.

He nodded and, putting his head in his hands, flopped into a seat.

I scurried around him to our tiny galley. I heated a can of thick, nourishing soup.

Then I had an idea.

In the galley was a box of sleeping pills. Not many had been used.

I glanced over at Captain Turner. He was still bent over, his head in his hands.

Quickly I broke open a half-dozen of the pills and spilled the white powder into the thick soup.

"Here's something for you to eat," I said as I brought the bowl over and placed it next to him. Almost violently, without bothering with the spoon, he grabbed the dish and drained it in half a dozen fast gulps.

How long would it take for the drug to work? An hour? Two hours? I didn't know.

I heated a meat-loaf dinner in our electro-oven and brought it to him. This, too, he seized and greedily pushed into his mouth, swallowing as fast as he could shove it down.

Silently I moved as far back in the cabin as I could, half-hiding behind the master control panel. All that I could do was hope he would fall asleep before he remembered I was still there.

For a long time he sat, bent over, mumbling and groaning, with his head in his hands. Then gradually he slid frontward onto the floor.

I hardly dared let out even a small sigh of relief. After several minutes I got up enough courage to go over and touch the captain's shoulder. He did not respond.

Now what to do? I had possibly saved myself for the moment, but I also knew that another danger was swiftly approaching. Within just a few hours we were supposed to be reaching Gaea. Perhaps this fact—after two years of suspense on the trip, losing his crew—had snapped Captain Turner's mind.

I had no idea how to operate the ship or how to land it. If only Captain Turner had stayed sane another day or two!

I went back and looked at the control-panel board. It had never been explained to me. All I could remember was that when one of the crew had asked about landing procedures, the captain had said it would be handled automatically. He said if any adjustments had to be made on landing, he would make them.

A truly automatic landing was my only hope. The control panel was a maze of buttons and levers and switches and dials. Even now, the dials were flashing wildly as they had never acted before.

Were we landing already?

I waited. I had no way to look out. There was an exterior observation system, but I did not know how to operate it. All I knew was that the ship was decelerating rapidly. The pressure on my body was all but unbearable.

I tied Captain Turner's arms and legs to the most solid objects in the cabin. Then I strapped myself into my bunk.

The braking pressure became an agony. My head felt as if it would burst. My flesh felt as if it were being pulled free from my bones.

Just when I thought I could stand no more, there was a violent jerk upward, and after swinging a few times the ship seemed to stop.

I peered over at Captain Turner. He was still just as I had left him.

One of the few things I had been able to learn about the ship was how to open the escape hatch. Unfastening my straps, I clambered up onto the upper deck of the ship and proceeded to go through the various steps required to get the door open. One by one the latches fell away, until at last I swung the hatch cover inward.

I had no fear about the air on Gaea. The original explorers had made a good analysis of the atmosphere and had reported it as almost exactly the same as on Earth.

I took a deep breath of the cool, fresh air as the door swung aside. Slowly and carefully I raised my head out into the open.

The first explorers had never actually landed on the surface of the planet. Instead they had flown low through many orbits. They reported they had seen a form of intelligent life—probably humanoid. But they had not wanted to risk a landing among them. That was to be the task of *Hermes VI*.

With my head now well out of the escape hatch, I looked about. It was as the explorers had stated—a lush, beautiful, promising land, rich with vegetation.

I let out a metal ladder that was there for that purpose. I climbed out and down.

After two years in the cramped confines of the ship, it

was wonderful to feel my feet touch ground again. I looked around. All was gloriously green. It was all and more than the explorers had said it was.

Then—suddenly—I knew that one of Gaea's creatures was behind me. My mind was "receiving" thoughts. I turned slowly.

It was not quite humanoid, for it was shorter and rounder than any human. It wore no clothing. Its head was hairless and large for its body. Its skin was quite red. Instead of arms it had what looked like eight or ten tentacles. It stood upright on two short, stubby legs.

But it was the face that held my attention. There were two eyes at the end of foot-long protruding extensions. A large, round mouth was apparently used for breathing. Winglike, flapping ears completed the picture.

The astonishing thing to me, however, was the overall expression of friendliness and goodwill. Here was a creature, I realized with relief, that meant me no harm.

For a moment I was stunned by the suddenness of our meeting. I collected my wits and with an effort tried to probe into the creature's mind.

With a shock I realized it was doing the same to me. Instantly we broke out into mutual smiles at recognizing that we could communicate. Not with words. But with thoughts.

Still smiling, I stepped toward the being and held out my right hand in a gesture of friendliness. One of its tentacles slipped around my hand and pressed all eight of my fingers warmly and gently.

I had a new friend. I felt it all through my being. And it felt good.

Then I thought of Captain Turner.

I turned toward my new friend and with amazing ease, from my mind to his, related what had happened. To my surprise he nodded that he understood.

Almost at the same instant more of the creatures

slipped around from the other side of the Earth ship. They stood looking at me with their strange, waving eyes. Without saying anything, four of them climbed the metal ladder. In a few minutes they were back, carrying the still-sleeping body of Captain Turner.

The Gaean, my new friend, sent a tentacle curling reassuringly around my shoulders. His thoughts streamed into me.

"You say your captain has a madness," he said with his mind. "We know about madness. Sometimes we can cure it. If we cannot, we will make sure he does no violence—to you or to us. You fear him and yet you wish him no harm. I can feel it. You have nothing now to fear—either from him or from us."

I nodded. There was no need to use words. He knew just how I felt. He knew I now felt not only safe, but truly happy, almost for the first time in my life.

I looked about at the natural beauty of Gaea. Whether or not Captain Turner ever recovered, this I knew was my new true home. Why should I ever consider going back to Earth?

I smiled at my Gaean friend as he led the way into the green forest primeval.

some are born cats

by TERRY & CAROL CARR

"Maybe he's an alien shape-changing spy from Arcturus," Freddie said.

"What does that mean?" asked the girl.

Freddie shrugged. "Maybe he's not a cat at all. He could be some kind of alien creature that came to Earth to spy on us. He could be hiding in the shape of a cat while he studies us and sends back reports to Arcturus or someplace."

She looked at the cat, whose black body lay draped across the top of the television set, white muzzle on white paws, wide green eyes open and staring at them. The boy and the girl lay on her bed, surrounded by schoolbooks.

"You're probably right," she said. "He gives me the creeps."

The girl's name was Alyson, and it was her room. She and Freddie spent a lot of their time together, though it wasn't a real Thing between them. Nothing official, nor even unofficial. They'd started the evening doing homework together, but now they were watching "Creature Features," with the sound turned down.

"He always does that," Alyson said. "He gets up on the television set whenever there's a scary movie on, and he drapes his tail down the side like that and just *stares* at me. I'm watching a vampire movie, and I happen to glance up and there he is, looking at me. He never blinks, even. It really freaks me out sometimes."

The cat sat up suddenly, blinking. It yawned and began an elaborate washing of its face. White paws, white chest, white face, and the rest of him was raven black. With only the television screen illuminating the room, he seemed to float in the darkness. On the screen now was a commercial for campers; a man who looked Oriental was telling them that campers were the best way to see America.

"What kind of a name is Gilgamesh?" Freddie asked. "That's his name, isn't it?"

"It's ancient Babylonian or something like that," Alyson told him. "He was kind of a god; there's a whole long story about him. I just liked the name, and he looked so scraggly and helpless when he adopted us, I thought maybe he could use a fancy name. But most of the time I just call him Gil anyway."

"Is George short for anything?" the boy asked. George was her other cat, a placid Siamese. George was in some other part of the house.

"No, he's just George. He looks so elegant, I didn't think he needed a very special name."

"Gilgamesh, you ought to pay more attention to George," the boy said. "He's a *real* cat; he acts like a cat would really act. You don't see *him* sitting on top of horror shows and acting weird."

"George gets up on the television set, too, but he just goes to sleep," Alyson said.

The cat, Gilgamesh, blinked at them and slowly lay down again, spreading himself carefully across the top of the TV set. He didn't look at them.

"Do you mean Gil could be just hypnotizing us to think he's a cat?" Alyson asked. "Or do you suppose he took over the body of a real cat when he arrived here on Earth?"

"Either way," Freddie said. "It's how he acts that's the tip-off. He doesn't act like a cat would. Hey Gil, you really ought to study George—he knows what it's all about."

Gilgamesh lay still, eyes closed. They watched the movie, and after it, the late news. An announcer jokingly reported that strange lights had been seen in the skies over Watsonville, and he asked the TV weatherman if he could explain them. The weatherman said, "We may have a new wave of flying saucers moving in from the Pacific." Everybody in the studio laughed.

Gilgamesh jumped off the television set and left the room.

Freddie's Saturday morning began at eight o'clock with the "World News Roundup of the Week." He opened one eye cautiously and saw an on-the-spot reporter interviewing the families of three skydivers whose parachutes had failed to open.

Freddie was about to go downstairs for breakfast when the one woman reporter in the group smilingly announced that Friday night, at 11:45 P.M., forty-two people had called the studio to report a flying saucer sighting. One man, the owner of a fish store, referred to "a school of saucers." The news team laughed, but Freddie's heartbeat quickened.

It took him twenty minutes to get through to Alyson, and when she picked up the phone, he was caught unprepared, with a mouthful of English muffin.

"Hello? Hello?"

"Mmgfghmf."

"Hello? Who *is* this?"

"Chrglfmhph."

"Oh, my goodness! Mom! I think it's one of those obscene calls!" She sounded deliriously happy. But she hung up.

Freddie swallowed and dialed again.

"Boy, am I glad it's you," Alyson said. "Listen, you've

got to come right over—it's been one incredible thing after another ever since you left last night. First, the saucers—did you hear about them?—and then Gil freaking out, then a real creepy obscene telephone call."

"Hold it, hold it," Freddie said. "I'll meet you back of the house in five minutes."

When he got there, Alyson was lying stomach down on the lawn, chewing a blade of grass. She looked only slightly more calm than she sounded.

"Freddie," she said almost tragically. "How much do you know?"

"About as much as the next guy."

"No, seriously—I mean about the saucers last night. Did you see them?"

"I was asleep. Did you?"

"*See* them! I practically *touched* them." She looked deep into his eyes. "But Freddie, that's not the important part."

"What is? What?"

"Gilgamesh. I seriously believe he's having a nervous breakdown. I hate to think of what else it could be." She got up. "Wait right here. I want you to see this."

Freddie waited, a collage of living color images dancing in his head: enemy skydivers, a massacred school of flying saucers, shape-changing spies from Arcturus. . . .

Alyson came back holding a limp Gilgamesh over her arm.

"He was in the litter pan," she said significantly. "He was covering it up."

"Covering what up?"

"His doo-doo, silly."

Freddie winced. There were moments when he wished Alyson were a bit more liberated.

Gilgamesh settled down on Alyson's lap and purred frantically.

"He has *never,* not once before, covered it up," she insisted. "He always gets out of the box when he's finished and scratches on the floor near it. George comes along eventually and does it for him."

Gilgamesh licked one paw and applied it to his right ear. It was a highly adorable action, one that never failed to please. He did it twice more—lick, tilt head, rub; lick, tilt head, rub—then stopped and looked at Freddie out of the corner of his eye.

"You see what I mean?" Alyson said. "Do you know what that look means?"

"He's asking for approval," said Freddie. "No doubt about it. He wants to know if he did it right."

"Exactly!"

Gilgamesh tucked his head between his white paws and closed his eyes.

"He feels that he's a failure," Alyson interpreted.

"Right."

Gilgamesh turned over on his back, let his legs flop, and began to purr. His body trembled like a lawn mower standing still.

Freddie nodded. "Overdone. Everything he does is self-conscious."

"And you know when he's not self-conscious? When he's staring. But he doesn't look like a cat then, either."

"What did he do last night, when the saucers were here?"

Alyson sat up straight; Gilgamesh looked at her suspiciously.

"He positively freaked," she said. "He took one look and his tail bushed out and he arched his back. . . ."

"That's not so freaky. Any kind of cat would do that."

"I know . . . it's what comes next." She paused dramatically. "In the middle of this bushy-tailed fit, he stopped dead in his tracks, shook his head, and trotted into the house to find George. Gil woke him up and chased him onto the porch. Then you know what he did? He put a paw on George's shoulder, like they were old buddies. And you know how George is—he just went along with it; he'll groove on anything. But it was so weird. George wanted to leave, but Gil kept him there by washing him. George can't resist a wash—he's too busy grooving to do it himself—so he stayed till the saucers took off."

Freddie picked up Alyson's half-chewed blade of grass and put it in his mouth. "You think that Gil, for reasons of his own, manipulated George into watching saucers with him?"

Gilgamesh stopped being a lawn mower long enough to bat listlessly at a bumblebee. Then he looked at Alyson slyly and resumed his purring.

"That's exactly what I think. What do you think?"

Freddie thought about it for a while, gazing idly at Gilgamesh. The cat avoided his eyes.

"Why would he want George to watch flying saucers with him?" Freddie asked.

Alyson shrugged elaborately, tossing her hair and looking at the clear blue of the sky. "*I* don't know. Flying saucers are spaceships, aren't they? Maybe Gilgamesh came here in one of them."

"But why would he want *George* to look at one?"

"I'll tell you what," said Alyson. "Why don't you ask Gilgamesh about that?"

Freddie glanced again at the cat; Gilgamesh was lying preternaturally still, as though asleep, yet too rigid to be truly asleep. Playing 'possum, Freddie thought. Listening.

"Hey, Gil," he said softly. "Why did you want George to see the flying saucers?"

Gilgamesh made no acknowledgment that he had heard. But Freddie noticed that his tail twitched.

"Come on, Gil, you can tell *me,*" he coaxed. "I'm from Procyon, myself."

Gilgamesh sat bolt upright, eyes wide and shocked. Then he seemed to re-collect himself, and he swatted at a nonexistent bee, chased his tail in a circle, and ran off around the corner of the house.

"You nearly got him that time," Alyson said. "That line about being from Procyon blew his mind."

"Next time we tie him to a chair and hang a naked light bulb over his head," Freddie said.

After school Monday, Freddie stopped off at the public library and did a little research. They kept files of the daily newspapers there, and Freddie spent several hours checking through the papers for the last several months for mentions of flying saucers or anything else unusual.

That evening, in Alyson's room, Freddie said, "Let's skip the French vocabulary for a while. When did you get Gilgamesh?"

Alyson had George on her lap; the placid Siamese lay like a dead weight except for his low-grade purr. Alyson said, "Three weeks ago. Gil just wandered into the kitchen, and we thought he was a stray—I mean, he couldn't have belonged to anybody, because he was so dirty and thin, and anyway, he didn't have a collar."

"Three weeks ago," Freddie said. "What day, exactly?"

She frowned, thinking back. "Mmm . . . it was a Tuesday. Three weeks ago tomorrow, then."

"That figures," Freddie said. "Alyson, do you know what happened the day before Gilgamesh just walked into your life?"

She stared wonderingly at him for a moment, then something lit in her eyes. "That was the night the sky was so loud!"

"Yes," said Freddie.

Alyson sat up on the bed, shedding both George and the books from her lap in her excitement. "And then that Tuesday we asked Mr. Newcomb in science class what had caused it, and he just said a lot of weird stuff that didn't mean anything, remember? Like he really didn't know, but he was a teacher, and he thought he had to be able to explain everything."

"Right," said Freddie. "An unexplainable scientific phenomenon in the skies, and the next day Gilgamesh just happened to show up on your doorstep. I'll bet there were flying saucers that night, too, only nobody saw them."

George sleepily climbed back onto the bed and settled down in Alyson's lap again. She idly scratched his ear, and he licked her hand, then closed his eyes, and went to sleep again.

"You think it was flying saucers that made all those weird noises in the sky?" Alyson asked.

"Sure," he said. "Probably. Especially if that was the night before Gilgamesh got here. I wonder what his mission is?"

"What?" said Alyson.

"I wonder why he's here, on Earth. Do you think they're really planning to invade us?"

"Who?" she asked. "You mean people from flying saucers? Oh, Freddie, cool it. I mean a joke's a joke, and Gilgamesh *is* pretty creepy, but he's only a little black-and-white cat. He's not some invader from Mars!"

"Arcturus," Freddie said. "Or maybe it's really Procyon; maybe that's why he was so startled when I said that yesterday."

"Freddie! He's a *cat!*"

"You think so?" Freddie asked. "Let me show you something about your innocent little stray cat."

He got off the bed and silently went to the door of the bedroom. Grasping the knob gently, he suddenly threw the door open wide.

Standing right outside the door was Gilgamesh. The black-and-white cat leaped backward, then quickly recovered himself, and walked calmly into the room, as though he had just been on his way in when the door opened. But Freddie saw that his tail was fully bushed out.

"You still think he's a cat?" Freddie asked.

"Freddie, he's just a little weird, that's all—"

"Weird? This cat's so weird he's probably got seven hearts and an extra brain in his back! Alyson, this is no ordinary cat!"

Gilgamesh jumped up on the bed, studied how George was lying, and arranged himself in a comparable position next to Alyson. She petted him for a moment, and he began to purr his odd high-pitched purr.

"You think he's just a cat?" Freddie asked. "He sounds like a cricket."

"Freddie, are you serious?" Alyson said. Freddie nodded. He'd done his research at the library, and he was sure something strange was going on.

"Well then," said Alyson. "I know what we can do. We'll take him to my brother and see if he's really a cat or not."

"Your brother? But he's an osteopath."

Alyson smiled. "But he has an X-ray machine. We'll *see* if Gilgamesh really has those extra hearts and all."

On her lap, George continued to purr. Next to her, Gilgamesh seemed to have developed a tic in the side of his face, but he continued to lie still.

Alyson's brother, the osteopath, had his office in the Watsonville Shopping Centre, next door to the Watsonville Bowling Alley. His receptionist told them to wait in the anteroom, the doctor would be with them in a moment.

Alyson and Freddie sat down on a black sofa, with the carrying case between them. From inside the case came pitiful mews and occasional thrashings about. From inside the office came sounds of pitiful cries and the high notes of Beethoven's Fifth. Somebody made a strike next door; the carrying case flew a foot into the air. Freddie transferred it to his lap and held it steady.

A young man with longish brown hair and a white jacket opened the door.

"Hey sister, hi Freddie. What's happening?"

Alyson pointed to the carrying case. "This is the patient I told you about, Bob."

"OK. Let's go in and take a look."

He opened the case. Gilgamesh had curled himself into a tight ball of fur, his face pressed against the corner. When the doctor lifted him out, Freddie saw that the cat's eyes were clenched shut.

"I've never seen him so terrified," Alyson said. "Weird, freaky, yes, but never this scared."

"I still don't understand why you didn't take him to a vet if you think he's sick," her brother said.

Alyson grinned ingratiatingly. "You're cheaper."

"Hmpf."

All this time the doctor had been holding the rigid Gilgamesh in the air. As soon as he put him down on the examining table, the cat opened his eyes to twice their normal size, shot a bushy tail straight up, and dashed under the table. He cowered there, face between paws. Alyson's brother crawled under the table, but the cat scrambled to the opposite side of the room and hid behind a rubber plant. Two green eyes peeked through the leaves.

"I think stronger measures are indicated," the doctor said. He opened a drawer and removed a hypodermic needle and a small glass bottle.

Freddie and Alyson approached the rubber plant from each end, then grabbed.

Freddie lifted the cat onto the examining table. Gilgamesh froze, every muscle rigid—but his eyes darted dramatically around the room, looking for escape.

The doctor gave him the shot, and within seconds he was a boneless pussycat who submitted docilely to the indignities of being X-rayed in eight different positions.

Ten minutes later Alyson's brother announced the results—no abnormalities; Gilgamesh was a perfectly healthy cat.

"Does he have any extra hearts?" Alyson asked. "Anything funny about his back?"

"He's completely normal," said her brother. "Doesn't even have any extra toes." He saw the worried expression on her face. "Wasn't that what you wanted to find out?"

"Sure," said Alyson. "Thanks a lot. I'm really relieved."

"Me, too," said Freddie. "Very."

Neither of them looked it.

"Lousy job," said Gilgamesh.

They turned to look at him, mouths open. The cat's mouth was closed. He was vibrating like a lawn mower again, purring softly.

Freddie looked at the doctor. "Did someone just say something?"

"Somebody just said, 'Lousy job,' " said the doctor. "I thought it was your cat. I must be losing my mind. Alyson?" —she looked to be in shock—"Did you hear anything?"

"No. I didn't hear him say 'Lousy job' or anything like that." Still in a daze, she went over to the cat and stroked him on the head. Then she bent down and whispered something in his ear.

"Just haven't got the knack," said Gilgamesh. "Crash course." He smiled, closed his eyes, and fell asleep. But there was no doubt that it was he who had spoken.

Freddie, who had just got over the first wave of disbelief, said, "What was in that injection, anyway?"

"Sodium pentothal. Very small dose. I think I'd better sit down." The doctor staggered to the nearest chair, almost missing it.

"Hey, Alyson?" the doctor said.

"Huh?"

"Maybe you'd better tell me why you really brought your cat in here."

"Well," said Alyson.

"Come on, little sister, give," he said.

Alyson looked at the floor and mumbled, "Freddie thinks he's a spy from outer space."

"From Arcturus," said Freddie.

"Procyon," said Gilgamesh. He yawned and rolled onto his side.

"Wait a minute," said the doctor. "Wait a minute, I want to get something straight." But he just stared at the cat, at Freddie, at Alyson.

Freddie took advantage of the silence. "Gilgamesh, you were just talking, weren't you?"

"Lemme sleep," Gilgamesh mumbled.

"What's your game, Gil?" Freddie asked him. "Are you spying on us? You're really some shapeless amoebalike being who can rearrange your protoplasm at will, aren't you? Are your people planning to invade Earth? When will the first strike hit? Come on, *talk!*"

"Lemme sleep," Gilgamesh said.

Freddie picked up the cat and held him directly under the fluorescent light of the examining table. Gilgamesh winced and squirmed, feebly.

"Talk!" Freddie commanded. "Tell us the invasion plans."

"No invasion," Gilgamesh whined. "Lemme down. No fair drugging me."

"Are you from Procyon?" Freddie asked him.

"Are you from Killarney?" the cat sang, rather drunkenly. "Studied old radio broadcasts, sorry. Sure, from Procyon. Tried to act like a cat but couldn't get the hang of it. Never can remember what to do with my tail."

"What are you doing on Earth?" Freddie demanded.

"Chasing a runaway," the cat mumbled. "Antisocial renegade, classified for work camps. Jumped bail and ran. Tracked him to Earth, but he's been passing as a native."

"As a *human being?*" Alyson cried.

"As a cat. It's George. Cute li'l George, soft and lazy,

lies in the sun all day. Irresponsible behavior. Antisocial. Never gets anything done. Got to bring him back, put him in a work camp."

"Wait a minute," Freddie broke in. "You mean you came to Earth to find an escaped prisoner? And George is it? You mean you're a *cop?*"

"Peace officer," Gilgamesh protested, trying to sit up straight. "Law and order. Loyalty to the egg and arisian pie. Only George *did* escape, so I had to track him down. I always get my amoeba."

Alyson's brother dazedly punched his intercom button. "Miss Blanchard, you'd better cancel the rest of my appointments," he said dully.

"But you *can't* take George away from me!" Alyson cried. "He's my *cat!*"

"Just a third-class amoeba," Gilgamesh sniffed. "Hard to control, though. More trouble than he's worth."

"Then leave him here!" Alyson said. "If he's a fugitive, he's safe with me! I'll give him sanctuary. I'll sign parole papers for him. I'll be responsible—"

Gilgamesh eyed her blearily. "Do you know what you're saying, lady?"

"Of course I know what I'm saying! George is my cat, and I love him—I guess you wouldn't know what that means. George stays with me, no matter what. You go away. Go back to your star."

"Listen, Alyson, maybe you ought to think about this . . .," Freddie began.

"Shaddup, kid," said Gilgamesh. "I'll tell you, George was never anything to us but a headache. Won't work, just wants to lie around looking decorative. If you want him, lady, you got him."

There was a silence. Freddie noticed that Alyson's brother seemed to be giggling softly to himself.

After long moments Alyson asked, "Don't I have to sign something?"

"Nah, lady," said Gilgamesh. "We're not barbarians. I've got your voice recorded in my head. George is all yours, and good riddance. He was a blot on the proud record of the Procyon Co-Prosperity Sphere." Gilgamesh got to his feet and marched rigidly to the window of the office. He turned and eyed them greenly.

"Listen, you tell George one thing for me. Tell him he's dumb lucky he happened to hide out as a cat. He can be lazy and decorative here, but I just want you to know one thing: there's no such thing as a decorative amoeba. An amoeba works, or out he goes!"

Gilgamesh disappeared out the window.

On the way back to Alyson's house, Freddie did his best to contain himself, but as they approached her door, he broke their silence. "I told you so, Alyson."

"Told me what?" Alyson opened the door and led him up the stairs to her room.

"That the cat was an alien. A shape-changer, a spy hiding out here on Earth."

"Pooh," she said. "You thought he was from Arcturus. Do you know how far Arcturus is from Procyon?"

They went into her room. "Very far?" Freddie asked.

"Oh, *boy!*" Alyson said. "Very *far!*" She shook her head disgustedly.

George was lying in the middle of the bed, surrounded by schoolbooks. He opened one eye as the two of them tramped into the room, then closed it again, and contented himself with a soft purr.

Alyson sat on the side of the bed and rubbed George's belly. "Sweet George," she said. "Beautiful little pussycat."

"Listen, Alyson," said Freddie, "maybe you ought to think about George a little bit. I mean, you're responsible for him now—"

"He's my cat," Alyson said firmly.

"Yeah, well, sort of," Freddie said. "Not really, of

course, because really he's an alien shape-changing amoeba from Procyon. And worse than that, remember what Gilgamesh said, he's a runaway. He's a dropout from interstellar society. Who knows, maybe he even uses drugs!"

Alyson rested a level gaze on Freddie, a patient forgiving look. "Freddie," she said softly, "some of us are born cats, and some of us achieve catness."

"What?"

"Well, look, if *you* were an amoeba from Procyon and you were sent off to the work camps, wouldn't you rather come to Earth and be a cat and lie around all day sunning yourself and getting scratched behind the ears? I mean, it just makes *sense*. It proves George is *sane!*"

"It proves he's lazy," Freddie muttered.

George opened his eyes just a slit and looked at Freddie—a look of contented wonder. Then he closed his eyes again and began to purr.

ROGER ELWOOD is a self-confessed "nut" about science fiction, fantasy, and ghost stories—in fact any story that has something weird, mysterious, or other-worldly about it. Mr. Elwood made a careful selection among the many well-known authors in the science fiction and fantasy field he has worked with over the years and commissioned them to write stories especially for this book. Mr. Elwood has written and edited more than thirty anthologies of science fiction, fantasy, and ghost tales.

THEODORE STURGEON is one of the deans of modern American science fiction. Over the last twenty years he has written countless science fiction novels and short stories. In addition he has written scripts for movies and TV including the *Star Trek* series.

PRINTED IN U.S.A.

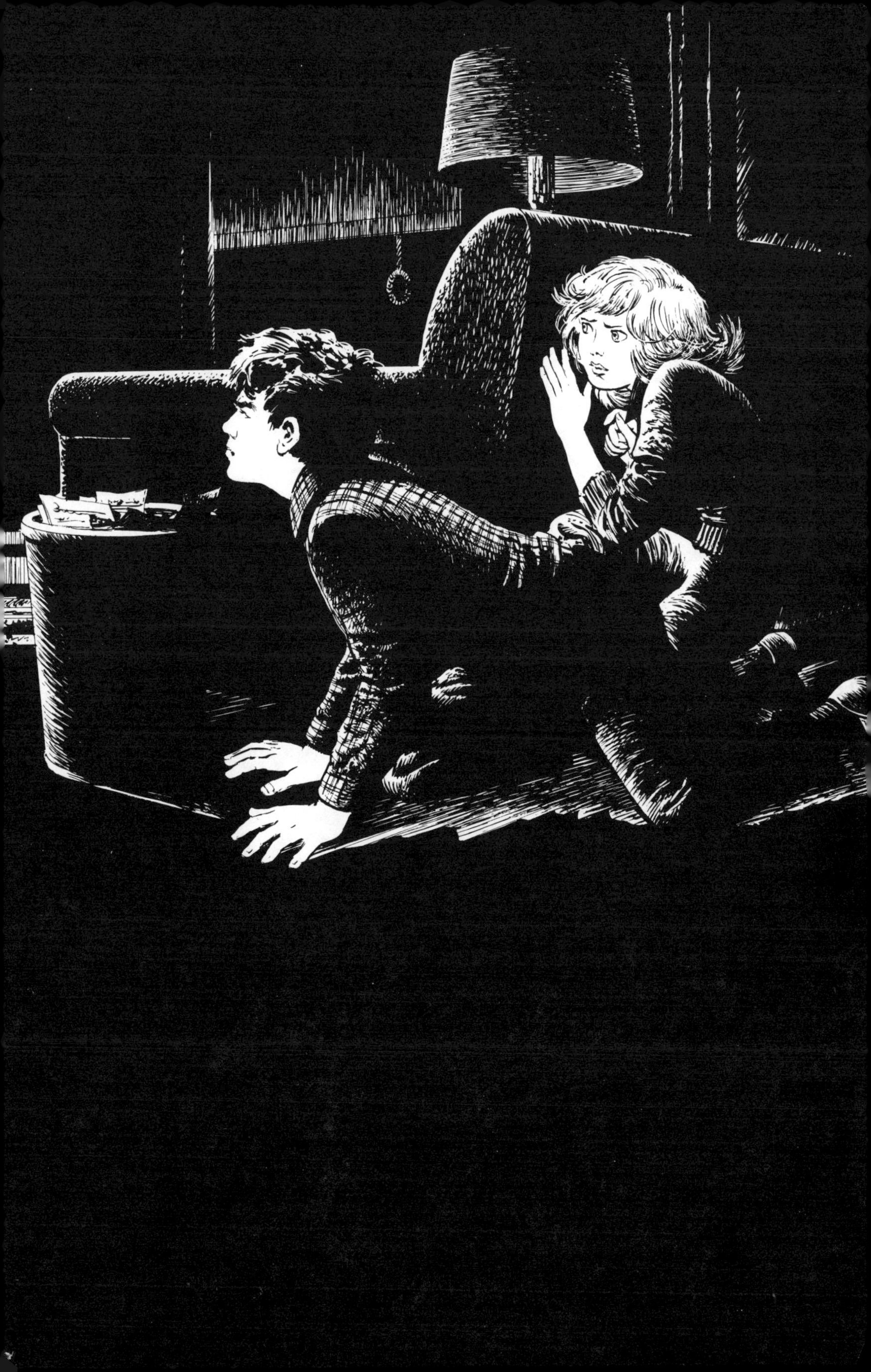